Georgina's
Christmas
Joy

BERYL WHITE

ROMANCE
PUBLISHING

COPYRIGHT

CONTENTS

1

THE NASTY SURPRISE

London, 1892

Life was not going well for Georgina Stockwell. One Friday afternoon, she found herself summoned to sit at the impressive oak desk at Wade & Bainbridge's Cheapside headquarters. Her gaze fell blankly on a thick brown ledger containing the woeful financial accounts for the historic family brewery business, Stockwell & Sons. Beneath the leather tome, the desk was plastered with papers outlining the repayment schedules for several sizeable loans taken out within the last two years. There was also a metal spike stuffed with a stack of unpaid invoices at the far end of the desk.

"As you can see, I had to say something," were the gentle words from her advisor, Mr Bainbridge.

With a nod, Georgina indicated her agreement. She didn't bother to glance up, but she could still see the expression on her solicitor's face. His tiny grey head looked down at his hands that were being relentlessly wrung to steady his nerves.

"I would have told you about this earlier," he said, "but your brother, Mr Duffield, promised me he would talk about it with you personally. He assured me some months ago that he would inform you of the gravity of the situation. I took his word for it. I shouldn't have, and I'm sorry."

"Yes," she croaked, her voice stolen by guilt and anger. "I'm afraid we all made the mistake of putting too much faith in my sibling, Mr Bainbridge. Me included."

She wanted to refuse to accept the gravity of the situation, but the facts were inescapable. James had known for a while that things weren't looking too rosy at the brewery. Debts were spiralling, sales were dwindling, yet James remained silent, ignorant, or both. Georgina had always believed that her brother wasn't the successful industrialist he liked to present himself as. It wasn't that she had let him off the hook, but rather that, as a woman, she would need hard evidence to prove her concerns that he had been mismanaging things for some time. Now, she was saddled with the problem of paying off his debts. It seemed, sadly, acceptable to assume a woman should be able to do that, but often not much else.

"What do you propose, Mr Bainbridge? Should I be planning my summer wardrobe for my trip to Australia at Her Majesty's pleasure?"

Mr Bainbridge removed his glasses and rubbed his eyes.

"Well, your late spouse may have some bonds that you could consider liquidating. That might make a small dent in the arrears. Show commitment to the lenders, if you will. But it won't be nearly enough to settle all the loans. Another option is asking the bank for additional time to repay them. Of course, even if they agree to play ball, you might be unable to keep your promise if you don't have enough income to meet the new payment plan. I wish there were another solution, but right now, all you can do is lay off workers."

"But that makes no sense? Surely production will suffer if there is insufficient staff? It might cease altogether!"

"I believe if you lowered your output on your more unpopular ales, you could limp along for a while longer."

"That helps with variable costs, but not my overheads. With declining output comes lower profits" Georgina frowned.

"I agree. But it is a stay of execution," Mr Bainbridge conceded. "We're like field doctors attempting to stop the casualty bleeding to death on the battlefield right now, Mrs Stockwell. We need to do something both temporary and effective until we can get more help. I can chase outstanding pub invoices and reduce your payment terms so that you can improve cash flow and pay your suppliers. Although that might take a week or two to take effect. Those are the final points I need to bring to your attention. Except for—" he wrung his small hands with vigour and continued to look at the floor.

"Go on, Mr Bainbridge."

"There might be some possessions you can sell, either personal or business, although this assumes you or your wider family have assets you can liquidate."

Georgina slumped in her seat as low as her corset would allow. The whalebones dug in, adding to her pain. London was enjoying an Indian summer, and the office was hot and stuffy. She felt like the walls were closing in on her. The whole situation was overwhelming, especially as she was stuck with a problem that was not of her own making.

The family business, which had been in the Stockwell's hands for three generations, had been inherited by her husband, Richard. A mere two years after the Lord took him, the company was on the verge of collapse due to the carelessness of her feckless brother. She hadn't wanted to hand the business over to him, but it was never supposed to be hers to run. Only the men in the family had that privilege.

She wasn't quite sure how James had done it, but it was clear the guarantor of the loans was her, not him. Making her the sole owner of all the risk had allowed James to take all the phantom rewards.

Her trusted advisor dropped his head as though he had done something wrong, even though he had done his absolute best for the business and her family throughout the terrible time of Richard's sudden and untimely demise. Mr Bainbridge didn't have a very high opinion of James, but he didn't think the cad would sink to fraud. He, too, was wrong.

His head snapped up when Georgina's palms thumped on the desk, making the papers bounce and waft.

> "It's not just me he has swindled, but all our hard working staff," she grumbled. "Those families have been with us for generations too."

"I am afraid redundancies really are your best option in the short run, Georgina," he suggested. "Here are some projections."

He tried to hand over a green cardboard folder stuffed with reams of calculations, but she didn't take it.

"I shall defer to your expertise, Mr Bainbridge. If you're sure redundancies are the best option, then that is what we must do. Please see that the workers affected are informed as they receive their wage packets at the end of today. They need to plan their futures too," she sighed.

Her surrender brought their conversation to an end. She left the offices, head held high, hoping that Wade & Bainbridge would do everything they could for her. She'd had a bellyful of men letting her down.

But as soon as she stepped out onto the pavement and the front door shut, she felt crushed, a complete failure. The weather was on the turn. The drizzle and the hot, humid smog were as suffocating as her woes. Each pair of eyes she encountered seemed to be judging her, blaming her for not having a backbone, not stepping in earlier, and for making sure hundreds would be left with empty bellies before the next week was out. And those were the lucky ones. The unlucky ones with no savings would be evicted by their landlords and be at the mercy of the workhouse.

She felt alone and defeated, and their opinions of her were entirely justified.

As she sat in the carriage, although the physical separation from the complex paperwork provided some respite, she was melancholic on the trip to her home in Milford Square,

Mayfair. Wanting to be alone to reflect on her changing fortunes, she asked the driver to take a meandering route. Worrying about the company's future, she felt just as complicit as James about how the business was being run into the ground.

Things were going to get worse before they got better. On her immediate return, she needed to get changed and head down to James's birthday party. Georgina's mother persuaded her to host a surprise dinner for him and his hedonistic friends. As usual, she did as she was told.

She despaired at the thought of spending the evening feigning she wasn't furious with her conniving little brother, surrounded by vacuous, self-serving women and arrogant men on whom he loved frittering away his—or, more specifically, her—money. She was also livid that the party would have been financed by her money.

When she arrived at her terrace house, every window was aglow against the inky black October evening sky. From the coach, she looked up at the decorative walls, the elegant pillars, and the wrought iron railings marking the second-floor balcony. She longed to slink in via the servants' door and crawl into bed unseen.

Her coachman hopped down from his wooden bench before she could decide whether to sneak in or not. Her eagle-eyed butler, Mr McKay, was there to greet her as soon as she stepped out, leaving no chance of escape. She hesitantly climbed up the two steps from the pavement. Inside, the house was a hive of activity, with maids buzzing around from room to room, making everything perfect for the evening's festivities.

"Good evening, ma'am," said Mr McKay, with his usual deep, slow delivery.

"Hello, Mr McKay. Can you send Sarah up to my bedroom with some hot chocolate? Before this evening, I fancy something sweet and sugary to calm my nerves."

"Nerves, ma'am? May I enquire as to what is troubling you?"

"No, you may not."

"Can I assist in any way?"

"No, please just ask for the chocolate. And be quick about it. I need to get ready for the party tonight."

"As you wish, ma'am," he said as he gratefully accepted her gloves, scarf, and bonnet.

She ascended the hallway's white marble steps, the smooth stone bannister slipping through her hand, passed through the gallery on the second floor, and headed up another flight of stairs to her bedroom. The servants were still bustling about her, finishing up the final touches. In greeting, they bowed and curtsied, and she returned the respectful gesture with a quick nod, but they seemed just as relieved to be leaving her presence as she was theirs. Georgina looked at all the decorations and thought about the exorbitant cost of the orchids and ice sculptures.

Desperate for a moment's peace, she stepped inside her bedroom, closed the door, and rested against it for a few seconds, eyes closed to shut out the horrors around her. She opened them to find that her lady's maid, Sarah, had already prepared her evening dress. Made of dark green silk, it had a scooped heart-shaped neckline and short puffed sleeves. She'd loved it during the fittings she'd had in spring. It was so lovely to be out of formal mourning attire. It had seemed special, but now it looked like another pointless waste of money. She had a wardrobe full of formal wear. Putting it on that night would be a real chore. All she wanted was to snuggle up with a hot chocolate in her tatty old pyjamas.

Just as she finished her chocolate, there was a knock on the door.

"Ma'am, are you ready to get dressed?"

"Yes," she lied.

Georgina waited patiently by sitting on the rose-coloured, velvet upholstered stool that accompanied her walnut wood dressing table. She looked at her tired reflection in the mirror.

How could it be that she had aged so much in just a few hours? She looked years older. Her rosy glow had been replaced by a sallow complexion. Her eyes looked puffy and heavy-lidded. Deep creases and dark circles underlined her soft brown eyes. In her mid-twenties, it was shocking that she looked so haggard and demoralised.

"Oh, Richard," she whispered to herself. "Please accept my apologies. I have let you and your family down terribly, and it's my fault."

"Everything alright, ma'am?" Sarah asked. "You look a bit subdued if you don't mind my saying."

"Oh, I'm fine, Sarah. It's been a long day, that's all."

Georgina looked at her Mayfair home with a critical eye, wondering how long it might take to sell and what would happen to all her loyal staff if she sacrificed it for the brewery.

2

THE GIFT OF THE GAB

Hours earlier, in the East End, life was well underway. The morning sky over London was yet to brighten. The city awaited the sun to peek its head over the grubby skyline. The Cavendish family's two-bedroom tenement flat had a view into the street, where the brouhaha of a new day dawning could be heard despite it being just gone five AM.

The destitute of London's East End had little option but to get up before dawn if they wanted to find gainful employment for the day. Jon Cavendish leaned over and examined himself in the cracked mirror that was set on the mantelpiece. He fixed his shirt's starched collar and combed his black hair. He hadn't bought a new or secondhand shirt in a very long time, and was still wearing the same pair of baggy trousers that his father had worn several years before. To their credit, though, they had been washed and invisibly patched.

Unlike most unskilled labourers, Jonathan Cavendish placed a premium on looking presentable. While he had lacked a permanent position for a while, he hoped to find such a role very soon. He didn't see quality clothes as an expense, knowing that he would have a better chance of securing a job if he presented himself in a neat, well-groomed, and respectable manner. His father had lived by this belief and imparted it to Jon and his brothers and sisters. They were grateful for the lesson. They fared better than a lot of other families in their building.

Confident that he looked his best, Jon halved the loaf of brown bread that his younger sister Rachel had baked the day before. The Cavendish family never ate store-bought bread. Their mother had taught young Rachel not to trust shop loaves. The flour frequently contained unwanted additives like chalk or toxic plaster dust. There were always stories in the paper about some poor sod getting poisoned and trading standards taking samples. Jon would be happy to give up his simple luxuries if it meant he could buy his siblings the more expensive, but higher quality bread flour.

He stooped down, a piece of Rachel's bread still stuck inside his cheek, to kiss Archie, five, and Maggie, three, who were both sound asleep. Rachel was out for the count too, but Jon refrained from kissing her. If he so much as touched her forehead, she would instantly wake. It was the downfall of being forced to mature prematurely. Already, she was wise beyond her tender years.

As Jon crept quietly towards the long hessian sack that functioned as their front door, his father came out of their shared single annexe room. David Cavendish blinked blearily, even though the place was dark and gloomy.

"I take it you're leaving, son?"

"Aye. I was wondering, are you on day shift today?"

His father yawned, "Yes, son."

"I see Rachel washed your work shirt for you."

David smiled warmly at the sight of his eldest daughter's silhouette on the corner cot. The regular rhythm of her breathing made the covers gently rise and fall.

"I don't know why she does it. Bless her. I always come back all sticky and brown, stinking of hops like all the other lads."

"Yeah, you may be just another bloke to the rest of the fellas at work, but to her, you're special. You're her pa. She'll always be her pa's little gal."

"Never was a more honest statement spoken, son. Anyway, sorry for keeping you. Best of luck in your job search! And be careful out there on those streets now, you hear me?"

Jon walked out of their top-floor lodgings and started walking down the squeaky, steep steps of his tenement block. The dwelling had been a lovely big five-storey family house until a local landlord, the unscrupulous Jimmy McGinty, got hold of it. It was butchered by his men, who hammered in lots of thin wooden dividing walls. Instead of one family, it could now take up to sixty lodgers.

There was still a hint of rain from the previous evening's storm. All night long, he and his dad had to sleep with their heads next to a saucepan, with water from the roof constantly 'plink, plink, plinking' into it.

He saw a few familiar faces and gave a cheery wave as he weaved his way through Whitechapel's narrow, dingy streets. A frail old Polish woman looking for a good hawking spot lost her footing on the cobbles and dropped her basket of bobbins and pins. Jon stopped to help her gather up her stock and dust herself off. His job-hunting route always led him towards the river and the ports, where he was more likely to find paid work, even just a day's labouring. As it was where most of the men in his area of East London went in search of employment, Jon constantly wanted to steal a march on the competition. He was always among the first to arrive, no matter the weather.

The Thames became an even bigger foetid cesspool after the rain. This morning was no different, following last night's deluge. As Jon got nearer, the pungent odour of the big old river filled the air. He reminded himself that things could be far worse. No matter how poor he felt he was, others would always be on the next rung down life's long ladder. At low tide, he would see the mudlarks, the scavengers who sifted through the sludge for anything of value, including bits of old rope, shards of sharp metal, and even human remains.

Some people thought it was sad that folks were forced to do such things to eke out a living, but it only fuelled Jon's determination to get better-paid employment whenever and wherever he could. Despite his harsh environment and lack of opportunity, he was an optimistic fellow. He was blessed with natural charisma and powerful, persuasive communication skills, which always came in handy—for work or pleasure.

So far, his wiles hadn't resulted in many permanent positions, but he was hopeful. He was both able and eager to supplement his father's stable earnings from the Stockwell & Sons brewery. Rachel also pitched in when she could by accepting laundress and seamstress work when it was offered. They all had to pull together to make ends meet, especially after young Maggie's arrival. It had been three years since their poor wife and mother had died as she gave life to the girl.

Jon got to his usual spot early, but strangely, the quaysides were already crowded with folks searching for a bit of casual labouring. Mr Sedgwick, the dock supervisor and well known Geordie, saw him from a distance.

"Eh, up, Jonathan. How's tricks?"

"I'm in fine fettle, thanks for asking," he replied as he bobbed and weaved his way to the front of a small bunch of men.

"Timed that well, Mr Cavendish. I was just going to offer this guy your wage for grafting today. But since you're a regular, the work's yours."

Jon's attention drifted to the man in question. A few years older than Jon, the man's shoulders sagged under the same stoicism that characterised all the East End's hardy male residents. Despite the stoop, he seemed sturdy. Jon noticed the man's expression reflecting his displeasure at his job being snatched away from him at the last minute.

"Mr Sedgwick, please. This fella was here for work before me. You know I'm not workshy, but I don't want to steal bread out of his family's mouths."

"So, you're turning it down, are ya?"

Mr Sedgwick's bristly black eyebrows sprang up.

Fast thinking was required of Jon.

"How about this? Me and my new pal here, well, we'll work the shift as a pair. We'll divide the money fair and square, half each. It's better than nothing, ain't it?"

Jonathan turned his head to seek approval from his new acquaintance, who seemed most unimpressed by the offer. The same could not be said for Mr Sedgwick, who was pleased to be getting two workers for the price of one.

"What are you up to, Jon Cavendish?"

"Fair cop. Here's the rub. A little bird told me that an early cargo on Stockwell & Sons's biggest ship will arrive this afternoon. These poor lads behind me will have all scarpered to find employment elsewhere by the time it arrives, and you'll need extra hands. Now, if I'm correct, what's in it for me is that you pay us a day and a half apiece since we'll be sticking around to accomplish work that should actually be done by four or five men. Bargain, innit? And me and laddo here, well, we get more cash."

His eyes twinkled, and he shrugged.

"We all win."

Even Jon's new acquaintance was starting to feel upbeat after hearing things unfold.

"By Jove, that silver tongue of yours, Jon Cavendish, will either make you rich or get you locked up," chuckled Mr Sedgwick.

"Let's hope it's the former and not the latter, eh?" Jon joked as he playfully elbowed the manager.

He nodded politely to his new companion, and the two strolled out onto the quayside to start unloading the waiting goods.

He dived headfirst into his task, pleased with the opportunity to exert himself. For Jon, nothing beat the feeling of coming home from a long work day to the comfort of a warm fire and red hot bowl of stew, knowing that you'd earned every penny of your wage packet.

As the shift wore on, he felt the local tavern call, and he planned to stop in on his way home later to quench his thirst. No more than one, mind you. That was the agreement he had with his pa. One pint when the family's food and rent was covered. He was pleased he'd had this chat over his evening meal the night before. His dad's tip-off was lucrative for them all. He hoped his dad could let him know about more cash cows like that.

As Jon hoisted another heavy sack onto his shoulder, he smiled to himself. Life was good.

3

'KEEP HIM OFF THE GIN'

Jon was in a good mood when he left the tavern. He was as pleased as he'd ever been, with a full pay packet in his pocket and a belly full of beers. Not even the rain that had begun to fall as he sidled home could dampen his mood.

Jon and Rory, his new workmate for the day, had moved considerably more than two men's worth of cargo—just as he had promised Mr Sedgwick.

First, there had been the grain ship, which was docked when he arrived. Then the colossal Stockwell & Sons ship arrived, laden with a gross of barrels of stout that was to be moved, ready to be shipped out on a barge. Mr Sedgwick had been highly impressed with Jon's foresight. Rory had been grateful for the extra work—and money.

Rory was still in the pub working on his next pint when Jon left. He'd had two because his workmate had treated him to a second pint as a thank you.

> "Make sure you get home before you drink all your wages, Rory, or your wife will string you up!"

> "Aye aye, cap'n," Rory nodded with a fake naval salute.

Soaked to the skin and keen to share his good luck with the family, Jon took the tenement steps two at a time and burst through the door. What greeted him on the other side, in turn, burst his bubble of joyfulness.

Rachel was bent over little Archie, who was nuzzling beneath the covers right up to his chin. She sat, stony-faced, her hands trembling, on the side of his cot. She wiped the lad's brow with a damp cloth. Her dark, expressive eyes had lost their sparkle. Tears took the place of the twinkles. In the far corner of the room, a reflective Maggie sat alone, still on her own cot, pushed right against the damp wall. Sombrely, she twisted the ears of her threadbare toy rabbit, whose scrawny body had been twisted repeatedly over many sets of hands through the years, as she watched.

Mr Cavendish was observing the heartbreaking events from his bedroom's entrance. He appeared hopeless and dejected as he slumped against the rotting wooden doorframe. His pipe cleaner arms were folded over his sunken chest, and his nervous right foot was tapping out a random rhythm.

Jon started his medical assessment right away. He walked across the room and touched the boy's forehead with the back of his hand. The lad was roasting. He noticed the breathing was laboured and raspy, and the boy's cheeks were a fiery crimson too.

"How long has he been acting this way?"

Silence.

"Tell me!" he yelled.

"Since about three today."

Rachel didn't turn her head.

"He'd been quiet as a mouse all morning, but he often does that. Then, around midday, I knocked up a quick meal. He barely touched it, to be honest. After that, he said he wanted to lay down and has been like this ever since."

Rachel's voice cracked, and Jon could tell what was going through her mind.

"Rachel, you're not to blame for this. Do you hear me? There was nothing you could have done."

"But I should'a known. Should'a checked."

For an instant, her chin trembled. But Rachel, being Rachel, closed her little fists and wiped her puffy eyes with her bony knuckles to stop further tears from falling. Jon looked at his poor younger sister, so tragically forced to be a mother when she was still a child herself. Duty and responsibility were squeezing all the happiness out of her.

She gave her father a sideways glance. David Cavendish didn't reply. Instead, he made his way to the central table in the room and slumped onto a worn wooden chair, the family's sole seating option.

"He'll be fine, pa. You'll see."

"It's not just that," Rachel whispered. "Pa's lost his job."

"—If you're pulling my leg?"

"I'm not."

Jon's gaze wandered across the room, looking to lock onto his dad's, but David Cavendish's eyes refused to meet it.

"I don't understand, pa? You've never skipped a day of work in your life? You didn't get mouthy with your supervisor, did you?"

"Wasn't just me, son. A big group of us got the bullet today. I heard that they've got money troubles, big 'uns. So, us fellas are out on our ears. They sent some puny little beancounter in to share the glad tidings."

"Money troubles?"

"Yeah, Mr Duffield's been spending it on partying as fast as the company makes it, I heard. Seems things ain't the same since Richard Stockwell died."

"This new bloke. Is his name James Duffield?"

"Aye,"

"You mean that toff with the red nose who prances around like a peacock? That Mr Duffield?"

"Yep"

"Good grief."

Jon recalled James Duffield to memory instantly. It was easy because he'd immediately loathed him at first sight. A couple times, when he'd gone to the brewery to drop off his dad's lunch or do a bit of labouring, he'd spotted James. They were like chalk and cheese, and the two didn't get along during their time together.

Compared to Richard, Jon saw the new manager as a pretentious, incompetent, fat idiot who drank on the job. The ogre seemed to delight in being imposing and authoritative, though no-one saw him as a true leader. He was a drunken fool. A failure.

The son's irritation increased as he considered the 'businessman's' role in driving the brewery into the ground. If he wanted to be reckless with his own money, that was one thing, but with company money—when it affected the lives of his employees—well, Jon saw that as utterly disgraceful.

> "What annoys me, pa, is the lives of good blokes
> like you are ruined by selfish, toffee-nosed berks
> like him! As long as he and that widowed sister-in-
> law are kept in caviar, it's all tickety-boo! Sod the
> rest of us!"

He'd never seen Mrs Stockwell, but he expected her to be every bit as fat, dull and selfish as her useless brother-in-law.

He snapped his mind back into the room. Getting angry with the management only hurt him. Nothing was going to change, no matter how much he protested. Right now, his family needed his undivided attention and support, not petty rants back at home.

He ran his fingers over Rachel's curly black locks, which reminded him of his own, his father's, and grandfather's.

> "Just give me a moment, and I'll go and fetch the
> chemist. I had a stonking day down at the docks

today workwise, so we can afford to get someone round to see little Archie."

"But what about the rent?" asked Rachel.

"Jeepers! When's that due?"

"Soon. Can you afford it?"

"Right now, I don't know. If we need additional time, I'll talk to Mr McGinty about it. For the time being, Archie needs to be seen by a doctor."

Jon headed out the door, rushing to the chemist. Thankfully, there was a doctor available, who agreed to come and see little Archie.

The doctor pulled the stethoscope from his ears as Archie continued to cough and wheeze.

"Seems like a nasty lung infection. This damp's not good for you, you know?"

The chemist was a towering, authoritative figure with a hardened workhouse-warden-like bedside manner. He recommended some affordable, homemade remedies, lots of fluids, plain easy-to-digest food, and for Archie to stay away from wet environments.

"No matter where we go in Whitechapel, we'll get wet. Even if we stay indoors, it's so damp here, you're guaranteed to get a soaking. Look at them holes in our roof, for starters."

After Jon asked the physician, he received a noncommittal shrug in response.

"The boy has to make it through the night to have a chance at survival. Here, this will help."

The doctor rummaged in his bag and brought out the tiniest tincture bottle. "One drop, three times a day."

Jon's whole wage packet went on the medicine and the doctor's bill.

Watching Archie thrash and cough was all that could be done at this point. Time ticked by as he watched Rachel perform her motherly duties as the rest of the family wished the night away. How incredibly unjust everything was. Rachel was not supposed to be the head of the household. She was supposed to be a little girl, a carefree fourteen-year-old girl.

His father, who had been sitting hunched over at the table for hours, barely moved. His head was still cupped by his gnarled hands. It was a relief that young Maggie had gone to sleep before the chemist came. At least when she was asleep, she wasn't fussing next to him being infected. There wasn't enough money to treat two patients.

Jon felt like a small cog in a big machine that was about to crush him to a powder. Usually, he wasn't the kind to dwell on the past or worry about the future, but it wasn't so easy this time. Seeing his family struggle was always like a knife through his heart.

When his mother was still alive, he'd moved further afield when there was no dockyard employment or if another man was selected to work first. Last Christmas, when, yet again, the family lacked enough money to buy any meat for supper,

Jon bartered a few days of hard labour with the butcher in exchange for some hens that had stopped laying.

In Jon's mind, nobody was ever completely helpless. There was always a solution. Yes, they might have to find a way to scrape by after his dad lost his job, but they would cope. Perhaps not so well while Archie was ill on top of everything else—and definitely not with their family of five about to become a family of four—but they would manage. Jon would make sure of it.

Jon's head sprang into action as he saw his family floundering under these cruel twists of fate. At first, it was a sluggish, almost hesitant notion that he was sure he should reject. But the more he thought about it, the more he knew it was their only hope.

It was such a random proposition that the chance of success and improving the family's dire situation was negligible. It did guarantee one thing—freeing him from his sense of hopelessness.

"I'm off out," he announced.

"Out?" Rachel asked hesitantly. "This late in the day? Where exactly?"

"You'll be fine, won't you, Rachel?"

"Can't you wait here at Archie's side till he recovers?"

"I can't. I'm so sorry. I must leave now. Pa will help you."

Rachel cast a suspicious glance at her brother, then looked at her father, who was staring vacantly at his youngest son.

"Just keep him off the gin. He's worried about us all. It'll pass. Storm clouds always do."

Rachel looked at her father with a patient, loving expression that made Jon think of his mother. A lump gathered in his throat.

"Do what you must, Jon, like you always do. I'll hold the fort here."

A pang of guilt silenced him completely.

He gently patted Archie's little head, leaned down to kiss Maggie's ebony hair, and put his hand on Rachel's skinny little shoulder. She shrugged it away in a temper.

He left his lodgings, stepped out into the cold, wet night, and moved forward determinedly.

The plan was simple, if most likely doomed. He would go to Mayfair to see Mrs Stockwell, see if she could talk some sense into her rogue of a brother, perhaps stop him frittering away money on women or the gee-gees or wherever it was going.

While it might not improve his family's position over the next few days, it would undoubtedly make him feel better if he could vent some of his frustrations. Besides, it probably wasn't even illegal to confront a toff and give them a piece of your mind? At least, not to the best of his knowledge, anyway.

4

THE FIGHT FOR
WHAT'S RIGHT

Jon had already paid a visit to the house of the late Mr
Stockwell, many years ago. Ah, that lovely house in the
upmarket Mayfair neighbourhood. Unlike Whitechapel,
Mayfair had no impoverished communities, rundown
buildings, or destitute residents. Jon's memory was as clear
as if the meeting had happened yesterday. He reflected on
the contrast between the Stockwells' comfortable standard
of living and his own pitiful one.

Once a year, when old Mr Stockwell was still around, the
business would throw a summer party in their back garden
for all of the senior brew masters and their families, and
David Cavendish was eligible to attend. Jon was just a slip
of a lad back then, but he felt confident he could find his
way back. He was well-versed in the layout of London's
districts and could judge the four-mile distance between
Whitechapel and Mayfair well. Plus, there were some
suitable landmarks like the British Museum and Smithfield
Market to guide him along the way.

There wasn't enough money to pay for a public omnibus, so
it would take almost two hours to fight through the Friday
night traffic and mountain of costermonger carts. Luckily,
all that time on foot looking for work enabled him to walk
briskly for hours at a time. Rainwater seeping in through the

holes in his boots was an annoyance, but nothing he couldn't handle. As his hat became more saturated, water started to seep down from the brim and around his eyes, making him blink furiously, but he didn't slow his pace.

With its immaculate streets and upper-class residents, Mayfair finally came into view. On the cobblestones, posh carriages rumbled by, while posh gentlemen accompanied by posh women sauntered along. They eyed him with suspicion, and a distinctive 'what brings you here?' expression. The men discreetly covered their pockets with their hands. The ladies clutched their bags even tighter. He was disappointed his motives were silently questioned, but felt it was quite understandable.

Trying to melt into the drizzly gloom, Jon walked along with his head down and hands in his trouser pockets. He strolled till he reached the white terrace buildings that held those few meals so long ago. He was sure they were the correct ones. They surrounded one of the prettiest little squares.

He hesitated at the curb. What if Mrs Stockwell was out? It was unlikely at this late hour as a widowed woman. It was also unlikely she'd moved. When the rent was overdue, or the landlord found a renter able to pay more, toffs didn't up sticks and do a 'midnight flit' as his people did. No, toffs stayed put in their glorious houses.

Jon was pleased that he'd convinced himself she was in. He was at a loss for what to do if she wasn't. Two quick steps led up from the pavement to the large flagstone that formed the floor of the grand entrance. It was flanked by two smooth, gently tapering pillars. Jon raised his gaze to the roof of the house.

Each and every window was brightly illuminated by the interior gaslighting. It looked like a most splendid residence. Jon decided Mrs Stockwell was keen to show she lived in a beautiful home inhabited by equally beautiful individuals.

His astonishment almost brainwashed him into giving up. He kept his feet on the ground by reminding himself that these people might be wealthier, but they were not better than him. On the whole, he thought people around these parts were vile and self-centred. The house was a shell to keep the lower classes out of the way so they could hold lovely parties to discuss how to keep the workers on the bottom rung of the ladder. Well, that was then, and this is now, he told himself. Time to stand up and fight.

He stepped out onto the porch with determination. He smiled as he saw the little label under the doorbell, which read: 'Stockwell Residence.' Then, his airborne leg was halted by an angry voice behind him.

"You there! Stop where you are. You'll be wanting the servant's entrance to get in."

Jon turned to see who had launched the attack and saw an older, well-dressed fellow walking by. Even though Jon had a higher vantage point in the doorway, the man still managed to look down his nose at him. Jon glared at the man and then turned his back on him.

"I am quite happy to have my discussion on the doorstep. I don't need to go inside to air my grievance."

The gentleman lurked in the shadows for a while, but the need to shelter from the drizzle clearly overtook his nosiness, and he left.

To calm his anxiety, Jon took a deep breath before raising a hand to rap firmly on the door, with a perfectly polished gold lion's head door knocker. After what felt like an eternity, the glossy black door opened, revealing a tall, stocky man with receding hair, who Jon recognised as the butler. The servant peered out at the visitor with bleary eyes, showing no sign of astonishment at seeing someone of 'his type' at the doorstep.

He dragged out his standard phrase:

"We never—ever—give to beggars."

To emphasise his point, he advised:

"You can get free meals at local churches and other community centres that support the deserving poor. Now, get out of here before I report you to the police."

As the door made to swing shut, Jon jammed his foot in the frame.

"I am not here to beg, old boy. I want to have a word with Mrs Stockwell."

"And I want you to go."

"I'm not going anywhere until I get a chance to talk to her."

"You will when an officer of the law moves you on. It can mean quite a long stretch for attempted burglary."

A struggle ensued as the butler fought to close the door, and Jon battled to keep it open.

In a final, desperate attempt, Jon yelled into the entrance hall.

"I need to speak with you, Mrs Stockwell. Just for a moment. Please? It's about your decision over at the brewery."

A faint, exhausted voice wafted from inside. She had hoped to rest after retiring from her brother's soiree. It was not to be.

"McKay, who the devil is there at this time of night? Has James forgotten his damned key again?"

"It's nobody, mi' lady," the butler groaned as he pushed against the door as Jon pressed on with his campaign.

"Today, my father was laid off from your brewery, Mrs Stockwell."

He stopped to see what her response might be. Suddenly, he felt foolish. What was bellowing into someone else's hallway going to achieve? If the boot was on the other foot, he wouldn't be persuaded to listen to a ranting lunatic at his threshold. No, they'd get their ears boxed and sent on their way.

Regretting trying to barge in, he began to wriggle his foot out of the way. It came as quite a shock when the tiny woman's voice called from within:

"Please, Mr McKay, It's alright. Let him in. Take him to the parlour, will you?"

"But, perhaps, madam—"

"I said, let him in."

The butler's expression had changed from the grimace when wrestling with the intruder, to his usual sullen demeanour. He then swept the door open and stepped back with dramatic emphasis.

"Please come in, sir,"

Jon looked around the well-lit entryway, with its white marble staircase, colourful wallpaper, and gaslit gold sconces. The house looked the same as he remembered it, just as it was when his mother was still with them and his father was full of hope for their future.

The walls above the winding stair-well were hung with paintings of grand landscaped vistas. They evoked the idea of being portals to distant mythical worlds. Jon's stomach growled as the enticing aroma of roasting meat drifted toward him. He'd never smelled anything so tasty.

In the middle of this opulent display of wealth, to him, Mrs Stockwell stood out as the most remarkable sight of all. As she glided down the staircase, she didn't even remotely resemble the shrew-like, frumpy, fat, bulbous-nosed version of her brother he had imagined. She was thin, liked delicate frills, and kept her hair perfectly styled. Most surprisingly, she was much younger than he imagined. Close up, she didn't look much older than him.

Her big brown eyes were the focal point of a porcelain-doll-like face. She had thick, full hair that was more wavy than curly. It was pinned sensibly with only a tiny adornment at the nape of her slender neck. Jon observed that her dressing gown, which was a muted blue colour, was snugly tailored at the shoulders and waist before flowing loosely in a river of pleats down her small frame.

She looked at him blankly, without the disdain of her butler or the condescending hostility of the man who had approached him on the street. Jon's anger subsided a little under that steady stare, but only a little. The consequences of her decision would continue to be felt in the family budget, until his father found alternative work. Master brewer positions were scarce. At his age, he would be lucky to get a day labourer's job loading Youngs' casks onto their delivery wagons. It was quite a contrast. This frail little figure before him could wield enough power to decimate hundreds of lives.

Jon's eyes were glued to hers.

His introduction had been well rehearsed throughout his walk.

"My name is Jonathan Cavendish. Today, I'll have you know, missus, my hardworking father, was fired from his position as master brewer. He's been there for most of his life and considers his colleagues and the company his extended family. He is devoted, dependable, and dedicated. He's never broken a rule or been disciplined for any misdemeanour in all the time he's worked for you. You've done a horrible thing by throwing him out. You've discarded him like a tatty old shoe, haven't you? He's a proud family man, and five of us depend on his wage to survive. I hope you're ashamed. And all because you and your brother want to syphon off all the profits for yourselves. It's nothing short of a scandal."

Jon felt slightly nervous now that he had relayed this out loud, but stood his ground. It needed to be said, after all. He could see that Mrs Stockwell was taken aback, but only just. She hid it well on her gentle face.

"What was I supposed to do? Today I found out there are significant financial obligations to be met. I have a string of creditors chasing me. Pubs have been late in paying. I had two options. Either lay off some of the men for a while or sack everyone for good and close down. Neither option would allow me to keep everyone on the payroll. I am sure you are aware that it would be quite improper for me to take over the business as a woman. I am a figurehead, just like the queen. This is not a mess of my making, Mr Cavendish."

Suddenly the flames in Jon's belly were reigniting, blazing brighter than ever.

"But you've still managed to salvage your posh Mayfair pad, holding onto all your expensive jewellery, fancy dresses, and other pleasures. So, what are a few honest men thrown under the bus now that you've funded your nice, comfortable lifestyle? 'You're alright, Jack!' as they say. You never had any right to that money. The sweat and toil of men like my father made that possible. They should be the ones with the luxuries, not you, swanning about all day at tea parties, playing bridge."

It wasn't his intention to sound so spiteful. A little spiteful, yes, but not crass and cruel. She did have a point. It was not a woman's place to oversee the family business, and living in her dead husband's home was not unreasonable. But when given a chance to vent, he couldn't help but let it all out. He was tired of the hard life. He was tired of seeing his family struggle. He was like a steam engine's boiler, the pressure building and building, the gauge redlining a little too long, then the rivets holding it all together, giving way. Someone was bound to get hurt.

Jon had trampled over her feelings with his comments. He could read that clearly in her face. He'd intended to defend his father, fight his corner for him, and use his silver tongue to fix things. Instead, everything felt worse.

"Now, that's enough of that, young man."

An older man burst in from the dining room and paced over to Mrs Stockwell.

"Are you alright, my dear?"

"Please don't fuss, papa."

"Who are you to insult my daughter like that?
Under my roof!"

"I have every right to be here!" said Jon in a shaky, rather than commanding voice.

"You've got to be kidding me, you rotten little oik."

When Jon turned around to plan his escape, the arrogant, goggle-eyed face of James Duffield was staring back at him. The sight of Jon, drenched to the skin and wearing patched clothes, left him speechless.

Jon's confidence was returning. He'd riled them. He'd said his piece. He looked at her once more and fired a farewell shot.

"All of you have something to be embarrassed about. You ought to feel ashamed of yourselves. You might think I am an idiot, but I am not. You have your academic knowledge, and I know how to treat people properly. I am more well-versed in the ways of the world. I know what it really means to be human, to fight to survive no matter what. You couldn't care less about anyone but yourselves. Your family will live forever with your wealth and status, and I'll die with my beloved labouring brothers in the East End. Without us, you'd have none of this!"

Then, he rounded the occasional table in the vast hallway, pushed past Mr Duffield, who was sputtering and yelling after him and made his way outside.

The rain had picked up to a constant pour. Big sploshes landed in the deepening puddles. Jon moved quickly with his head bowed, looking over his shoulder every few steps to make sure no police officer was after him.

As he progressed, the streets deteriorated and eventually merged into the rundown, filthy, and congested areas frequented by society's lowlifes. With a sigh of relief, he was happy to be back where he belonged.

By the time he returned to his family's tenement, it was well past midnight. He looked up to the top floor. His father was still up and about inside, worrying about Archie. He was pleased to see him less melancholic and able to look after his younger brother. The lad seemed to be making some progress, though Jon was realistic enough to know the young 'uns often rallied before fading away, ready for the Lord to take them.

While Archie's fever was abating, he wasn't coughing while he slept and his breathing was far less laboured. Although still fully dressed, Rachel lay on the blankets in her cot. Her sleep was deep and uninterrupted. She must have drifted off watching him.

"Back then?" said his father, with less of a question, more of a statement.

Jon slumped into the one chair at the table.

"Aye. I have to say, I don't think that went terribly well."

"What didn't?"

A guilt-ridden Jon turned to his father.

"I went over to Mrs Stockwell's."

David stopped tending to his younger son, and turned his attention to his eldest.

"Tell me you didn't! You're pulling my leg, aren't you?"

"Sorry, pa. I had to. Someone had to stand up for this family—and all the others. Things needed to be said!"

"Heavens! What needed to be said? Yes, we had the chop, but I wanted to leave the door open. And I've not had my references yet! You daft fool. You'll have made it worse, not better!"

Jon rolled his eyes.

"So, it's alright for them to be living the life of Riley, while we can't afford the medicine for Archie or to put food on the table?"

"Tell me you didn't bleat about how hard life is! Name-calling like a sissy. We have managed. We will manage. We don't need pity!"

Jon was tired of his father's timidity, tired of having to bow, scrape, and pander to rich overlords. He looked in the cracked mirror and noted he was tired of everything.

"I didn't call anyone anything. Not that it matters. You don't work for them anymore. They fed off your loyalty and hard graft for years and left us with nothing. Not even a thank you note for your long service."

Jon had had enough of talking, so he trudged to bed without wishing his pa goodnight.

He'd set out to unburden himself, to stick up for his hardworking dad, to confront Mrs Stockwell, and he'd done that. He told himself it was better than fuming about his father being treated like a doormat—except the rabble-rousing rant hadn't brightened his mood. He only felt more defeated, hopeless, and overlooked than ever before.

What was to become of the Cavendish family? At the moment, it seemed nothing good.

5

LIFE AND DEATH OF THE PARTY

James's soiree petered out soon after Jonathan Cavendish's unwelcome intrusion. The atmosphere wasn't exactly sizzling to begin with. It lurched along while everyone waited for James to make an appearance. He arrived way past fashionably late, and had clearly stopped at a few pubs on the way. He was drunk, and not particularly entertaining. With Mr Cavendish's ranting, the atmosphere was ruined. The soiree ended early, as each guest made their apologies and left.

At the end of the evening, four souls remained. Georgina, her parents, and her odious brother.

"No wonder there were so many problems at that place, James, if that's the kind of person you hired to work in your factory?" Mr Duffield chided.

"No, pa. But—''

"That man was an uncouth lout! Is he one of those who still has a job? I think you should fire him right away."

"He was standing up for his father," Georgina countered.

"What will the neighbours think? A common labourer shouting the odds in our hallway?" snapped her mother.

"Mother dearest, it is hardly the scandal of the century. 'Man raises his voice by a door'."

"No respectable man would want to marry a widow who allowed that sort of carry-on."

"Silly me. It's only been two years since my husband died and I still haven't found another Prince Charming" Georgina rolled her eyes in a sarcastic kind of way.

"That's a dreadful thing to do to Richard's memory. That's what concerns me," said James, trying to shame his sister.

"I have no intention of getting married again!"

She looked like the whistle on a steam train, her face hot and her mouth stiff and angular as she tried to ignore the provocation from her sibling. James stood back with a horrible smirk as Mr and Mrs Duffield hurled abuse at her.

Georgina let the words wash over her. She had made a terrible mistake when she let James manage Richard's business. He was far too self-confident, loved the sound of his own voice, and bathed in his self-importance. Her brother needed his wings clipping. Her attention floated back into the room. The argument had turned nasty.

"—He ought to be put to the gallows for his rebellious views. If a monarch can lose his head, so should a liberal rebel!"

"—Even the workhouse is too good for those ruffians!"

Georgina refused to listen to her parents' constant criticism of the less fortunate, but now was not the time to try and reason with them.

When they eventually left for their own homes, she dragged herself wearily upstairs, reluctantly allowing Sarah to undress her before hiding under the covers. It would be a long wait for sleep's glorious respite from her earthly troubles. Even then, sleep could help not her. Nightmares stalked her unconscious mind. Like a visit to Scrooge, the visions were painful lessons. Jonathan's steely gaze followed her wherever she tried to flee. Her conscience pursued her even more vigorously.

She had disappointed herself. She had disappointed him, betrayed her loyal workforce, failed them—and there was nothing she could do or say to make up for it. She cried out in her nightmare, desperate for guidance. No one came to help. Not even the fire brigade when the building had been torched by the disgruntled workers. In the end, the brewery was destroyed. In the wake of the destruction lay the proud Stockwell family's history. A history that had stood the test of time until James's meddling brought it crashing down. Disowned by her own family, only Georgina and a mound of bricks remained. Waking in a flap, Georgina never wanted to sleep again. She sat up and wiped the beads of sweat from her brow, thinking about Jonathan and his too true words. She sank back down into her pillow, wondering if she could make things right. Eventually, though, exhaustion claimed her, giving her only two hours of rest.

She had wanted to start the day fresh, with a mind to solve some of the problems, but her brain was sluggish, and her heart was heavy with shame. Sarah brought her a cup of tea. Sipping at the refreshing brew, hope began to dawn on her. The seed of an idea grew as she picked out some clothes with Sarah. While she ate her breakfast alone at her table, with a statuesque footman standing in the corner, the seed grew into a formal plan, a plan to liquidate some assets. It was an unusual, even unfortunate, solution, but it seemed like it was her only choice.

6

THE RESCUE PLAN

Her first stop was the bank, where she presented the paperwork she had compiled from the study. As soon as that was complete, she made her way to Mr Bainbridge's office on Seacrest Street.

Although the wiry little man was slightly surprised by her sudden appearance, he was utterly taken aback when she gave him the portfolio with the fresh batch of paperwork. He nervously brushed his fingers across his temple as he perused the new documents. His expression was mainly one of shock, though Georgina felt she also saw a hint of melancholy. Feelings of remorse were also present. And maybe even some begrudging acceptance (or was she just imagining it?).

"Your rural retreat?" he deduced, still horrified. "I didn't anticipate you to give up your country estate when I advised you to review your asset holdings. That residence has been in the family of the late Mr Stockwell for many generations."

"I am aware of that, but beggars can't be choosers, Mr Bainbridge."

Her advisor put down the leather portfolio.

"Mrs Stockwell," he sighed, "you could have retired comfortably with the money you made from selling the brewery instead. Selling your country home in a rush will never attract a good offer. I would rather you hold onto it."

"My actions were in line with my duties, Mr Bainbridge. I believe we can agree on that. The profit from the labourers' toil footed the bill for the country house. Everything that went into making it, from the bricks to the stones to the furnishings, was paid for with brewery profits. Which would Richard have preferred I give up first? My own comforts, or my responsibilities to care for the loyal family men who made that lifestyle possible?"

She waited for a moment for her advisor to process her viewpoint, then continued.

"The domestic staff will remain in their current positions but will be paid for by a new master. But the brewery staff will struggle to find new roles. Yes, it is sad to lose such a wonderful building, but it is sadder to know the lives of hundreds would be ruined for the sake of my nice view of the countryside."

He admired the action and praised her.

"I believe that is a daring move, Mrs Stockwell."

"I can't deny it is a wrench, of course."

"The company may be able to stay afloat for long enough for this to be the saving grace, but I have to warn you, Mrs Stockwell: you can't rest on your laurels. Most of the debts can be paid off with the money you've raised today. But don't forget that there is a significant underlying problem that causes all of this in the first place. I can't put my finger on why the company isn't as lucrative as it used to be. It will take a lot of effort on your part to figure it out."

"Yes, I fully intend to get my hands dirty, as it were. No longer will I entrust James with this business. It is mine to run now. For the good of the men."

She rubbed her hands together excitedly.

"On that note, Mr Bainbridge, I need you to do two things for me. Please send a courier to the homes of all the men who were let go yesterday. Tell them they have been re-hired. I will personally bear the expense of their downtime, of course. Just tell me how much is owed. Have the couriers tell them also that they are to report to my home promptly at noon tomorrow if they wish to resume their employment at Stockwell & Sons."

"At your residence?"

"Yes. At my residence."

"But why not at the brewery? Would that not be a more appropriate place to meet your staff? They're a scruffy bunch, most of them. And some might be of questionable character. I suggest the housekeeper locks away all the valuables. I don't know whom Mr Duffield has hired since he assumed control. I couldn't vouch for any new men not there when Mr Stockwell passed."

"Good grief. I don't expect you to vouch for them," Georgina responded. "But my Richard and his father before him treated their employees like family. I'm sure you recall many successful luncheons and gatherings at our home. Those workers were invited into their lives back then, and my workers shall be invited into my life now."

Mr Bainbridge was about to protest, but Georgina put a finger on her own lips, using the gesture to silence him.

"If any fellow should turn out to be of questionable character," she advised, "we can decide what to do with him at that time. But for now, I need them to feel trusted and valued. If my rescue plan is to work, I need them to be invested, body and soul, in turning the brewery around with me."

"As you wish."

After the shock of the first favour, Bainbridge was hesitant about asking what else was on his to-do list, but protocol compelled him to speak up.

"And what is the other favour?"

"I need you to find the address of a Mr Jonathan Cavendish, immediately. His father was one of the men let go yesterday, and he came to see me at my home to give me some harsh words. I wish to find him and have this out with him."

"Have what out? Are you sure?"

"Absolutely. Snap to it. I intend to visit today."

"Oh, Mrs Stockwell, I have a bad feeling about your knee-jerk reaction. You must have a chaperone, surely? That part of town is, shall we say, 'salubrious'? It's not for a lady of your status to wander about alone."

Georgina pressed her two forefingers together and then rested her chin on them.

"Mr Bainbridge, I do appreciate your concern. But I intend to go. And I will go. And I'm going today. I have pondered what Mr Cavendish said and wish to reply to his grievances whilst his words are still fresh in my mind. Now, the address, if you would be so kind."

Five minutes later, Georgina had the information requested. She raced downstairs and hopped into her coach, which was soon rumbling its way over to Whitechapel.

"What a surprise visit this will be," she muttered.

7

NOT QUITE MAKING ENDS MEET

The night was dark and depressing when Jon returned from the quay. As always, there was plenty of work for everyone, but because Jon was early, he was assigned the most lucrative opportunity. Despite having a full-wage packet tucked discreetly under his shirt, he felt no joy from it. As he trudged wearily home, he realised that despite his hard work, he still felt unsatisfied. And he had no interest in popping for a pint at the Little Drummer Boy. Now he was the single breadwinner, and every penny counted. There would be no treats for him for a while.

He wished that his father would get a job soon. They could hardly get by on only one income, especially since it was only day work and not a permanent wage.

It was encouraging that Archie's fever had finally subsided. Most of the night had been spent close to him, with Jon on a bedside vigil, just in case it helped. Archie was fidgety and restless. Jon tucked his brother's sheets when he kicked them off. He sponged his brother's forehead and convinced him to drink some cold tea, so Rachel might get some rest. While his decision had helped his sister, not getting enough shut-eye to feel refreshed during the day had contributed to his dissatisfaction in the evening.

He stumbled along for what seemed like an age until he reached the cluster of streets he knew. He didn't have the patience to walk round to the main courtyard entrance, so he slid down the tiny back alleyway and off to the stairwell. He was lost in thought, dreaming of a cup of steaming hot tea, when he nearly tripped over Rachel and Mrs Tucker, who was visiting on the front porch.

He panicked. Was Mrs Tucker comforting Rachel? Was Archie alright, or had he taken a turn for the worse?

Jon took a deep breath, trying to steady his nerves.

"Is there a problem, Mrs Tucker?"

Like most women in Whitechapel, the mother of four, who looked much older than actual years, greeted him with a warm, gappy grin. Her forehead and eyes were deeply wrinkled and ingrained with dirt, yet her face was caring. Having a kind heart was something poverty could never dampen.

"Not really, Jonathan."

"Not really?" he asked, concerned.

"The only thing is—"

Rachel interrupted with a sly smirk on her face.

"—Seems you have a toff here to see you."

His brain clashed and clanged as he made sense of the comment. Not James Duffield, surely? Or is one of his cronies from the soiree coming to tear him a strip off for barging in like he did?

"A toff, you say. Well, I better go in and see him. We'll soon have this sorted."

He leaned down and kissed Rachel's head swiftly, then bounded up the five sets of stairs to his lodgings. His lungs and thighs burned, so he took a moment to gather himself. After taking a deep breath of bravery, he relaxed his face into a neutral look, then pushed the heavy hessian sack to one side, ready to meet whoever was on the other.

He was about to say Duffield's name and then stopped. Mrs Stockwell was perched on the one rickety wooden chair the family owned, which he had sat on as he watched Archie. She was telling the young boy a story she had been told as a child.

The lad had settled his grubby little head on his pillow and nestled inside his covers. Even though he seemed worn out, he observed the woman with rapt attention, as captivated by her beautiful voice as he was by the tale.

On hearing the footsteps, Georgina paused, and both sets of eyes turned to him in unison.

Jon let the sack on the door swing back down.

David stood by the edge of the table, his hands clasped behind his back. He seemed unnatural and stiff, as if he wanted to be motionless to try to hide his low status, but he was not happy about doing so.

Two cups of tea with slight chips in the rim were placed in front of him. One cup was his favourite one, so Jon presumed that Mrs Stockwell had been designated the other.

It was in better condition too. Maggie lay in a cot not far from Archie, sleeping soundly.

Rachel returned and sat on a blanket by the hearth, continuing her needlework to avoid the woman's piercing gaze, but she only had half an eye on what she was doing. Jon knew his sister well enough to surmise that she resented an adult woman's intrusion into her domain but was too respectful of her conspicuous wealth to show her displeasure. Mrs Stockwell indeed had an air of affluence, and if he was being honest, she looked fantastic. Although she lacked obvious beauty, there was something about the innocent 'girl next door' look about her face that was appealing. She was slight and slender and had soft skin, unlike the leathery-faced washerwomen of Whitechapel.

He stopped his reverie, disappointed that his anger was melting. The woman had just dismissed his father. She didn't deserve any kindness or understanding. She was just like the other toffs and 'only out for themselves.' His relaxed body language became more bristly.

"Ah, Mr Cavendish. How good to see you."

Her greeting came across as cordial, but her expression suggested nothing.

"Mrs Stockwell," he replied with the same wariness. "This is a surprise—A pleasant one," he added quickly.

Her face softened a little at the mention of the word 'surprise'. Surprise was just the reaction she had wanted.

"I'm here to see you and your father. But first, you must wait. I must finish my story."

Laughing, she ran her fingers gently around Archie's belly. A tired little squeal accompanied the boy tensing his stomach and turning away to escape the affectionate tickling.

Jon walked across the room and stood by his father, keeping a watchful eye on their unexpected houseguest while Mrs Stockwell continued her tale.

"That was a wonderful tale," Archie rasped quietly, his throat still raw from all the coughing and the lack of sleep.

"I agree, young man. It's one of my favourites, too."

"Can you tell me another?"

"I think perhaps you ought to get some rest whilst I chat to your brother and father."

She gently moved the black locks of his clammy white forehead and placed the woollen blanket back under his chin, then she joined the two men at the dinner table.

As their gaze locked, Jon felt his stomach lurch. Her stare seemed to have an underlying seriousness about it. If not seriousness, then something is definitely different. It was as if she could look beyond the tatty clothes and the depressing surroundings and see the measure of the man who stood before her.

All the posh folk he'd ever met before hadn't given him the time of day, preferring to think of 'his lot' as invisible. His class were unwashed, unbearable, an unwanted nuisance that were only tolerated because they provided cheap labour.

Her presumed compassion and empathy knocked him off his stride when it came to finding the right words to control the situation.

"Now, Mr Cavendish, senior and junior, I assume it is a mystery why I am here, a mystery you would like resolving?"

"Well, yes," said David. "Me and my boy here, we haven't done anything wrong. Perhaps me more than the boy, ma'am. I can only apologise for him gate-crashing Mr Duffield's birthday party—"

"—Allow me to interrupt you there, Mr Cavendish. I'm not here to argue or throw about blame. Heaven knows I was startled by your son's appearance on my doorstep last night and by what he had to say, but there's nothing to worry about. He was looking out for his family, and his actions took a lot of guts."

The two men looked on open-mouthed. She looked at Jonathan.

"The truth is that you had a very valid point. I should have to account for my choices and their effect on other people, in this case, many. You were also very wrong."

"Wrong?" Jon said, looking as if his hackles were rising.

"Yes, wrong. You made two errors of judgement. Firstly, you accused me of being selfish when I laid off most of my staff. I might be guilty of being small-minded or lazy, but not selfish. And I lay the blame for that with my advisor. Laying off workers was the only solution presented to me. Now, before you aim your sharp tongue in his direction, he is normally a good and competent professional, so I'll not have you criticising him."

Jon looked like he was about to criticise anyway, but he relaxed his shoulders and backed down.

"He applied standard accounting principles based on one misguided assumption."

Which was?" asked David.

"He assumed I was not prepared to sacrifice my personal wealth to save the brewery. That was his mistake, albeit understandable, I'm sure you'll agree. After your visit last night," she said, looking Jon in the eye, " I recognised the error. Who was I to take away the incomes of so many men and families, to take the food out of the bellies of households like yours, just to keep my life on an even keel? So, you see, I was lazy and small-minded. But it wasn't selfish. I was unaware."

Her eyes turned to her former master brewer.

"But now I wish to correct that mistake. I want to fight for the business. I want to fight for your families."

"But how can you fight for us? Since Mr Duffield's tenure, the brewery has been on its knees."

She ignored his point.

"As such, I would like you to return to my employ, Mr Cavendish. I want you to take up your old position for the same money. Starting tomorrow."

The eyes of David Cavendish widened. Like his father, Jon was stunned, but he managed not to show it.

"What about the other chaps?" Jon asked.

"I've had couriers send messages inviting them to have their old jobs back. That's assuming they will return. I appreciate I have a lot to do to regain their trust."

Jon found his ears ringing with astonishment. Could this be true? Having stomped over to Mrs Stockwell's home in her posh district and torn her a strip off in her own hallway, had he made a difference?

"Forgive my impertinence, ma'am, but why did you send a courier to the other staff but tell my father in person?"

Her lips curled upwards in a slight, smug grin.

" The reason I came here was not just to see your father."

"Oh?"

"Quite. You said some harsh home truths about the business and my part in it last night. I am glad you did."

"Glad?"

"Yes. It brought to my family's attention what a rotten job my brother has been doing as the manager. Additionally, you mentioned that I should not have given up so easily in their eyes. That opened the door for me to act. Yet, while I want to fight tooth and nail for my business, I am unsure how to solve the brewery's problems. In truth, I have no idea what those problems are, but I know they go far beyond debt."

"As you know, being a woman in charge of the business poses certain issues. I need someone to be my advisor, my enforcer. Someone I can rely on to act in the workers' best interests, and translate what's happening on the factory floor into words I can understand. Someone to explain my situation to them—so that together we can take the steps needed to save this business. Now, you can write me off, think of me as a toff who doesn't care, or you can help. Which is it to be?"

Jon was thrilled by her eyes, glinting mischievously at the prospect of proving everyone else wrong, proving that she could save the family business.

"So, are you in? Or out?"

"Before I agree, Mrs Stockwell, you told me I made two errors of judgement. What is the second one?"

She met his roguish smile with a wry one of her own.

"Your statement was that I preferred frills and luxuries to keeping good loyal men in work."

"In my defence, you had just sacked them!"

"True. But as it happens, I hate girly frills. Gentlemen, I bid you farewell."

She turned on her heels and swept out onto the landing before either man could ask if she needed an escort back to her coach.

"How's she going to get Mr Duffield to step aside, pa?"

"No idea, son. But I think she'll find a way."

8

OVERFAMILIARITY

The following day at noon, Jon and David returned to Mrs Stockwell's Mayfair residence. As soon as they stepped inside, the vigilant eyes of a large, portly man, Mr McKay, followed their every move. Despite the butler's watchful glare, Jon and his father's welcome was more respectful than they'd expected. The man managed to hide his undoubted undercurrent of revulsion well.

"Ah, gentlemen. Mrs Stockwell is expecting you."

Mr McKay took their battered coats.

"May I invite you to join the rest of the family in the drawing room? This way, please."

"I'll tell you one thing, mate: You're a dab hand at your job," joked Jon, cordially slapping the man on the shoulder so hard that the butler's head jerked.

David looked horrified by his son's overfamiliarity, but the man took it well.

"Thank you, Mr Cavendish. That is a point on which we concur."

Jon's spirits were lifted after his banter with Mr McKay. The hint of a smile formed as he followed his father into the living room, but it soon melted away as he realised what was waiting for him. A group of workers from the brewery were milling about, whispering to one another as they saw the two newcomers arrive. How amazed they were to be snacking on tasty little morsels from pretty porcelain plates. Some sipped at wine, sherry or port from tiny cut-crystal glasses. It was a far cry from their usual 'pie and a pint' fayre. David and Jon wondered what it would be like to nibble on such delicacies as they felt their stomachs growl. It was a painful reminder that neither of them had eaten since the night before. Only Rachel, Maggie, and Archie ate the half-a-loaf left for breakfast.

Two footmen in full livery and white gloves made their way through the crowd carrying trays of more refreshments. The two interlopers tried to behave as though the gathering was nothing out of the ordinary, but it definitely was.

The drawing room was opulent. The plum tones in the flowery wallpaper matched the decorative oriental rug covering the parquet floor. Each of the four walls was adorned with large oil-painted portraits of the Stockwell family, each framed in a colossal gold-leaf frame. An elegant fireplace stood on a white marble plinth, containing a cheery, crackling fire.

A chaise-longue and several chairs were available, but no one seemed interested in using them. Jon decided they were vacant because the men were uncertain about the occasion and how to behave, or were worried about leaving a mark on the immaculate plum-and-ivory striped upholstery.

David Cavendish stepped out from behind Jon to join the closest group of men in their cordial but awkward banter. Jon tagged along behind, but since he didn't know anyone, he hovered around on the periphery. Discreetly, one tall, haggard-looking man leaned in towards David to ask a question.

"What d'ya suppose this is all about, then, Dave?"

Jon thought it looked like the man's unkempt, greasy hair had been combed flat when he had left home, but now it was rebelling and sticking out over his ears. Jon wondered why he hadn't bothered to wash it properly beforehand.

"Well," said David. "All I know is that we've been reinstated."

"How come?"

"Mrs Stockwell visited our lodgings yesterday."

There was a gasp.

"She did? But why?"

"I just got a letter," grumbled one man.

"She came to offer a role to our Jon."

"So, she actually visited you in Whitechapel?" the tall man murmured.

Jon nodded.

"So, tell me, what's going on here?" a third asked.

"I don't know," snapped David.

"I do," announced Mrs Stockwell. "Please follow me to the library, gentlemen." She smiled generously at them all.

"Mr McKay, please make sure no one gets left behind," she added.

"Ma'am".

The men trooped along behind Mrs Stockwell, whispering.

"I came here on Friday night," said Jon, as he ran his hands through his thick locks and looked sheepish. "I laid it on the line saying how could she live here, in this swanky place, whilst the workers would probably end up in the workhouse."

All eyes were on him. The men's expressions ranged from shock to appreciation.

A short, stocky guy with one big tooth spoke up.

"You never did that, Cavendish, did you?"

"Course he did," whispered the tall man. "Everyone knows he's got a gob on him."

"He needs to learn to mind his gob. That's what he needs to do," said David.

"What exactly are you upset about, pa? My gob helped you get hired again, didn't it?"

"Come along now, gentlemen," Mrs Stockwell piped up. "There's no time for chit-chat. Keep up."

The men strolled down the corridor in a sheeplike procession, clearly unsure of what to do. Some men still had their canape plates and glasses with them, and others had left them behind. No one knew who was in the right and who was in the wrong.

"In here, if you please," said Mrs Stockwell in her best matronly tone.

In the library were tens of folded wooden chairs set out in a neat semicircle, three rows deep, gathered around an impressive walnut and leather reading bureau. Mrs Stockwell took her place at the desk.

Her hair was pinned back, and she was dressed sensibly in a dark grey dress, a plain waistcoat, and a high-collared white shirt (with no frills, Jon noted) underneath. As her visitors sat down, she brushed her skirts with her hands. Her brown eyes flickered from face to face, and when they landed on Jon's, her chin lifted ever so slightly, as if his presence gave her more confidence. She looked smaller than he remembered. As he observed her, Jon's stomach gave a sudden flip. It caught him off guard.

Jon and David Cavendish sat at one of the far ends of the last row. Jon felt out of place among the brewery workers, with such strong bonds forged over hundreds of shifts. As the chairs filled up around them, many men cast sceptical glances in his direction. Since he was old David's son, no one voiced their concerns directly.

Mrs Stockwell clapped her hands to grab their attention.

"Gentlemen, settle down now, please."

Her sudden inhalation beforehand told Jon she was just as nervous as them. His stomach fluttered again as he admired her courage. He told his gut to quieten down.

"Let me begin by expressing my most profound regret for last week's unexpected layoffs. According to my business adviser, Mr Bainbridge, all of you have accepted my offer, which makes me very happy. Thank you for putting your trust in me and putting the past behind us. I will never again make a rash decision like that, without exploring all options. You have my word. Moreover, I will pay for your time today to attend this meeting. You will not be out of pocket for not attending the factory today."

The men spoke amongst themselves and shifted in their seats as they briefly discussed the kind offer.

"Now," she barked, to regain control over the noise, "I will not gloss over the problems we—I— face at the brewery. It appears my sibling, Mr James Duffield, has run up enormous debts for the business."

"You only just worked that out, luv?" snapped a lanky man, before several others shushed him for his insubordination.

"Seems like you got a lot to learn," said another.

Georgina ignored the heckles and continued her review of their dire collective circumstances.

"Although I have paid off most of his obligations and been granted extensions on the rest, the underlying issue remains: sales aren't as good as they used to be. Profits are down. I wouldn't even hazard a guess as to why that might be. This explains your being here today. To reverse the brewery's downward trend. I'm hoping you can assist me in pinpointing the issues, and we can fix them together. Mr McKay, can I trouble you to take the meeting minutes?"

Her eyes met theirs with anticipation, but their gaze was one of mistrust. How could a woman solve business problems like these?

"Does anyone have an idea?"

When no one made a move, she hesitated.

"—Anyone? Come on, now. I understand from my advisors that many of you have decades of experience with the firm. Now's the time to speak up."

Her question was met with crickets.

Jon felt terrible for Georgina. It can't have been easy to stand before these strange men, pleading with them for assistance. She didn't seem the sort to be playing the victim. Not only that, but she was subjecting herself to this torture to help them and their families. She could have sold the brewery and moved on.

She continued to beg them to help, but they kept quiet, since a toff had never asked them for their opinion before. Jon knew they had plenty of opinions. Over the years, his pa had shared a lot about Richard Stockwell's solid management style, and James Duffield's woeful one.

When the men continued to be silent, Jon got to his feet.

"Excuse me, ma'am."

They locked glances for a split second. He recognised appreciation and optimism in her eyes, followed by an encouraging nod. He took in his surroundings and the assembled troops, looking to him to use his gift of the gab to solve the impasse.

"Some of you have known me since I was a little babe on my dad's lap, but if you don't know me, my name is Jonathan Cavendish. David Cavendish is a master brewer at Stockwell's and has been for many years. Although I don't officially have a job at the brewery, I do help out occasionally, mainly down the docks shifting the firm's cargo off ships. Pa has been working there since before I was born, and he's often talked to me about working there. I have a bit of an understanding, but not as good an understanding as you fellas."

He waited a moment for his words to register before continuing, so the men might be more willing to follow his argument.

"Men, this is your profession, not mine, and you have been given a once-in-a-lifetime opportunity to shape how this brewery works. How many other firms around here ask their staff their opinions? None. Now, Mrs Stockwell has confirmed the business is failing, but you didn't need her to tell you that. I reckon you figured that out for yourselves ages ago. If you're anything like me and me dad, you've complained to your loved ones during dinner. After a hard shift, you've had a bit of banter with a barman and a few locals. Ain't ya?"

The men nodded and laughed begrudgingly as Jon delivered his home truths.

"Tell me this? When has a stuck-up toff—begging your pardon, Mrs Stockwell—ever cared about what us lot think? When have they ever asked us for our thoughts? Nah, we are seen as stupid people. Slackers. Expendable. You know, and I know, you lot understand this business far better than any posh bloke wandering round with his cufflinks and clipboard. Now, you're being given a chance to speak up and shape your destiny. Don't waste it, men. Loosen those tongues of yours."

There was more murmuring.

"Yes, you there," he ordered, pointing to one chap. "You seem to have a lot to say to your neighbour. What's your take on this? Speak up, man!"

He glanced at Mrs Stockwell. The glimmer in her eye had changed. It was no longer gratitude; it was something he couldn't quite identify. Something much more alive. It was rather thrilling but also worried him.

The chair creaked as the man Jon had singled out rose to his feet. He fumbled with his cloth cap in his hands to steady his nerves.

"Well—it seems to me—Mrs Stockwell, that there's a problem with the stills." he began cryptically.

"Which is?"

"Well—please forgive me for this—but two out of the three are rusting inside. We took Mr Duffield to see them. Opened up the inspection hatch and showed it to him with his own eyes. But he did nothing. That was a year ago. Told us to just send a lad in there with a wire brush to sort it. The thing is, that would do nothing. We need new stills."

"Thank you, Mr—?"

"Watts"

"Does anyone else have an observation?"

"The engineering stores are a shambles. I've been patching machines up with bits of sheet metal from the scrap yard over in Stepney. Course, they don't have the parts we need, so I have to get cheap a labourer to hammer it roughly into position, then we weld it on like a seamstress patching an old coat. Patching doesn't matter on a coat, but it does when you've got to keep a machine watertight. There are so many leaks. And those day labourers, well, they don't care much. Not one of them gives that metal a scrub before working on it."

"Yeah. I've had to get metal from some of me mudlarking mates" said a small man in agreement.

Another guy chimed in.

"Mr Duffield had us scrape back up the most recent consignment of grain that was shedded off the wagon."

"And why is that a problem, sir? Did some of the sacks split?"

"Er, well, yes, ma'am. But the real problem was what it fell in. There was—er, a load of fresh horse muck on the floor. Landed square in it, it did."

"Oh!" said Mrs Stockwell.

"I mean, we did our best to pick out the good stuff, but there's a difference in taste, you know. And it's a bit gritty from the mud too."

Mrs Stockwell flinched at the thought of that. Her loathing of James grew a little stronger, which she didn't think possible.

"Hops, too," a new voice chipped in. "We've got a mould problem down there. One of my pals down at the docks told me Mr Duffield bought some of the cheap stuff that had fallen overboard. Ever since we stored that, even the good stuff has gone musty in the damp wintery weather. The hop store isn't heated properly. The windows are always misted up in the mornings this year, and the hops are in big sacks. It just turns to slime. There's more wrong with the hops store, but we'd be here all day."

"Yeah, and it's not just us who Duffield rubbed up the wrong way. He was rude to lots of the buyers. I heard him arguing with people in his office. And there was lots of argy-bargy with the distributors, delivery drivers, and the like. Put 'em right off working with us."

Jon kept a close eye on Mrs Stockwell. Her hopes dwindled as soon as the guys trotted out grievance after grievance, but she appeared to do her best to be upbeat. The home truths were shared for a good thirty minutes. Obviously, she had no idea how awful things had become at the brewery. Mentioning Duffield's name triggered a relentless unleashing of vitriol.

The woman sighed in relief when the men had concluded their lengthy list of concerns.

"Thank you, gentlemen. That was most illuminating. Mr McKay, please give me your notes. Before you leave today, I wish to summarise the list and for us to create one priority for each division. Believe me when I say that Mr Duffield is no longer employed by Stockwell's. I am taking over all senior managerial responsibilities with immediate effect. From now on, I demand that you come to me to update me on your progress and all your problems and worries. I intend to visit the brewery in person tomorrow. I'd like to get together so you can explain exactly what your problems are to me. Brace yourselves. I suspect it may be a very long day. Now, before you leave, please collect a food parcel from Mr McKay. Rather than provide you with luncheon, I thought some extra nourishment for your families would be more welcome."

The workers started trickling out of the Stockwell residence after the meeting concluded. Mr McKay helped the men into jackets and gave each one a brown paper bag packed with fresh food and a few tins. It took quite a while for the room to empty. Jon waited with his dad, neither of them in a rush to get back.

One of the maids pulled Jon to the side.

"My mistress wondered, might you and your father perhaps remain behind for a little while longer?"

"You tell her it's not a problem, miss," said Jon.

When Mrs Stockwell came to greet them, David's head was swivelling round, his attention going from one opulent object to another. Discreetly, she reached out, placed her soft, warm palm on Jon's arm, and smiled. Through his shirt fabric, he felt a thrill from her touch. He gazed at her slender, ivory hand before she pulled it away. He could barely look her in the eye. Jon willed the last of the men to hurry up with stuffing their arms into their coats and be on their merry way.

"Shall we return to the drawing-room?" she asked.

The two men nodded and trotted obediently in line behind her, like pages behind their monarch. She settled onto one of two armchairs across from the sofa. She sighed and looked down at her lap as her hand pulled at the pleats in her long skirt.

"Honestly, I wasn't sure what to make of today's session."

"It went well, ma'am," David counselled.

"And giving them some food to take back, well, everyone knows the way to a man's heart is through his stomach. The lads thought that was very generous of you. Their families will appreciate it."

"Well, I suppose that's one problem solved, hunger. The meeting was quite galling. I had hoped the problems had been more to do with James's abrasive management style. It seems not. The stills are corroded, the machinery poorly maintained, the working practices questionable, and the business relationships ruined. The only thing that seems to be working is the fabric of the building itself!"

The men didn't have the heart to tell her about the leaking roofs and crumbling outbuildings.

"Surely you can fix those. I think the men want to support you," David chimed in.

Jon had a lot of affection for his dad. He loved him deeply. However, his pa's thinking was often simplistic.

"The thing is, pa, even if the lads fix the building, Duffield managed to alienate all the good buyers, the distributors, the bars. And not only was he rude, but the quality of the ale has plummeted. We all know that they consider Stockwell & Sons beer not even fit for animals. They don't want to waste money on an ale they know their drinkers won't touch with a barge pole. It's not enough to make the factory work properly again. We have to get people trusting Stockwell ale again. Get them to give us another shot, which will be tough, given how badly they've been treated. I won't lie. It's going to be an uphill slog, pa. And that's if we don't trip and tumble on the way up."

David Cavendish lowered his head and slouched.

"It is a lot to take in," Mrs Stockwell admitted. "But it doesn't have to be a slog. I have no stomach for the climb. On the contrary, I am keen to start, and I am sure the view from the top will be worth it. And the climb will be a lot easier with your son with us. Oh, Mr Cavendish, Jonathan here is our secret weapon."

"He is?" said David, looking a bit stunned.

"Yes,

"I freely admit, although I knew your son's verve would be useful to this project, I wasn't sure how, but I am sure now. You, Mr Jonathan Cavendish, will be my spokesman. Your charming way with words will repair the relationships my brother sullied at all levels. Not just the workforce, but the suppliers, distributors, public houses, the drinkers, even, if it comes to that."

She paused, looking directly at him with her hazel brown eyes.

"This business meant the world to Richard and his forefathers—and now it does to me. Will you accept?"

Once again, there was tension in her voice, but now in a good way. Before, it was nerves. Now it was eagerness and expectation. Her enthusiasm was contagious. She was correct. Persuasiveness was instinctive for him, but it was never something he considered would become a profession. He thought back to his back-and-forth negotiation at the docks with Mr Sedgwick, when he had brokered an excellent deal for him and Rory. The thing was, that was an unexpected opportunity that he exploited. The idea of being able to unleash his talent on demand in a wide variety of scenarios, from the boardroom to the factory floor, felt daunting. Imposter syndrome was about to take hold until he took a wider view.

He'd plenty of experience with his gift of the gab. Mrs Stockwell had no experience running a brewery, yet here she was, fully behind the boldest change she would ever have to make in her life. If she was willing to take on the risk, so could he.

"If I am going to be a businessman, I better start doing this."

He leaned forward, thrust his hand into hers, and shook it vigorously.

"See, just like a proper business transaction. I'm learning. We've shaken on it to seal the deal, Mrs Stockwell."

"Georgina, please," she corrected softly, clutching his hand for a few seconds longer than expected in polite company.

9

THE COMMITMENT

Georgina stared at her mirror in the morning, wondering who the person was who looked out at her. While Sarah was on her hands and knees buttoning her boots, she struggled with her waistcoat's hemline.

"Do I look presentable, Sarah?" she asked her lady's maid.

"You look lovely, ma'am," replied Sarah calmly.

"I don't mean 'lovely'. I mean, do I look like someone in charge? Someone who knows what they are doing?"

"Always, ma'am. Those who know you well here recognise your competence. And your new staff will realise that about you too—if they take the time to get to know you."

"I hope they will afford me that time, Sarah."

"They will. There. That's your boots done. What's next?"

Georgina never lost her composure under pressure. Even when her husband was dying, she remained serene and organised. But when the going got tough, she needed a sounding board, a confidante. Sarah's straightforward, reassuring demeanour was always there. In terms of dependability, the woman was as solid as a rock, and it was appreciated. Her presence was soothing. That said, she was a bit of a 'yes man', tending to agree without too much scrutiny, so as soon as she left the room, Georgina's worries circled round in her mind again.

Looking in the mirror again, she pulled at her clothing, deep in thought. As evidence suggested, she decided that she had made a good impression on the men yesterday. She reasoned that David and Jon would have warned her if she was on a sticky wicket. The food parcels were an olive branch. Then she froze. What would happen if she got to the brewery and discovered she was in over her head and, in a panic, showed herself and everyone else that she was floundering. She regretted saying she would visit the premises today. There was no time to gear up on anything she was unsure of. The library was full of textbooks, but there was no time to read them, not properly, anyway.

Since Richard's death, she had seldom visited the place, and her memories of the layout were hazy.

She had very little visual recall of the premises since it had been Richard's family business, his passion project, not hers. She didn't give it much of a second glance when she visited, preferring to go straight to her husband's office. Given the rancorous relationship between her and James, and the sadness of seeing the place without Richard's cheery presence at the helm, she only visited once more after her beloved soulmate died.

The surprise visit from Jon Cavendish accomplished more than just preserving his father's career. It had woken her up to the idea that she wanted to preserve Richard's legacy and look after his loyal staff, who had supported him through thick and thin. It was the right thing to do, and she was going to find a way to do it, by golly.

Life had become stale as a widow. Mourning had forced her to become like a caged bird. The prospect of the cage door opening and liberating herself was exciting, if daunting. She looked at a photograph of her and Richard. Although captured years ago, it was as if his smiling face was willing for her to succeed at that moment.

She pushed her doubts aside and focused on the good that would come from her labours. Few women would get such an opportunity. She owed it to them to make the most of it. She had never realised how much she lacked in her life of late, until she found a way to put her time and energy to good use, and positively influence the world.

As she nibbled on a piece of toast, Georgina felt as if time was dragging and flying past at the same time. Still, she was eager to start, yet terrified.

Then it was time. Mr McKay informed her that the coach had been parked in the driveway and was ready for her. There could be no more prevarication, only action. She cocooned herself in her cloak, but the fear could still penetrate it and wrap itself around her soul. Her mouth was dry. Her hands tingled. There was the soft crack of some reins on a horse's back, followed by a lurch and a rattle as the vehicle headed off towards Whitechapel.

Throughout the journey, Georgina dreamed of being hidden in her bed, under the covers, safe. The enormity of her task filled all her mind in an instant, quicker than a paint brush could cloud a jar of water. Is that what she actually intended to do? Attempt to run a company about which she understood next to nothing?

Looking at the concerned face in the window, she thought, *'I don't even drink ale.'* Behind her reflection, London's majestic buildings whizzed past, bathed in buttery yellow sunlight. It was as if the Lord wanted to assure her everything would turn out well. At least, that's what she told herself.

When the carriage finally pulled up to the brewery, she looked and felt better than she had done earlier in the journey. Gazing up at the massive red-brick building that had been the pride and joy of Richard's ancestors was comforting, as if their spirits were waiting inside for her, wishing her well.

"It's time. I can do this," she said to no-one as she stepped out into the courtyard in front of the factory.

"You'll be fine, ma'am," said the coach driver, who had overheard her secret confession.

He pointed to the communication panel on the roof that was wide open. Georgina sent a pained glance back. The man, who introduced himself as Glazer, seldom conversed with her, but she could see a broad grin forming under the brim of his hat.

"I appreciate that," she whispered sincerely.

She strode confidently beyond the wrought iron gates, emblazoned with the "Stockwell & Sons" signage, and through to the goods inwards yard. As soon as she arrived, she sensed a thick malty odour clinging to her as she tiptoed across the muddy cobblestones. Sarah had insisted she wear her sturdiest boots. It turned out to be excellent advice. Even though the yard was only about twenty feet square, it served as a boundary, a threshold. Like some sort of simple yet challenging African ritual that transformed a young boy into a man. Crossing through the pair of solid oak doors that stood on the other side would change her life forever, taking her from a helpless widowed spectator to a successful entrepreneur.

She put one foot in front of the other, step by step, bit by bit, until her transformation was complete. She shoved her slight hands on the heavy wooden doors with all her might. There was no going back now.

10

THE NEW BOSS

To all the workers' amazement, 'the new boss' was there. Really there. Of course, some men pretended she wasn't there and carried on with their work, seemingly not skipping a beat. Others nodded in appreciation that she had kept her word. The remainder stood and stared open-mouthed. It was clear everyone had been filled in on the latest developments. It was a relief she wouldn't have to do a formal address to four times the number of men. Yesterday had been daunting enough.

She walked with purpose towards the administrative area. The only thing that gave away her nerves was her fiddling with the hem of her waistcoat again. She took the steps that led up to the right-upper side of the building. Richard's office, which was now her office, featured large windows that offered a spectacular vista of the factory floor. Like Richard's forefathers, she would have a bird's-eye view of all the staff as they worked.

Once again, she worried about how they would adapt to working for a woman, if at all. James had mistreated them so badly that they had every right to be disillusioned.

Later, as she walked across the brewery, she kept an eye on them. Everyone there seemed competent and productive. Each individual appeared to be an integral cog in a vast machine. In that part of the building alone, the brewery must have employed seventy or eighty men, not including the casual workers brought in to handle large flows of goods inwards or sizeable shipments. None of them stood idle. They were all working diligently, their muscular bodies grafting away as the sweat from their toil drenched them.

Even her inexperienced mind could see that every man was needed in that production area, and it would have been madness to trim the workforce to a skeleton staff. She was confused and angry about why Mr Bainbridge could imagine the business would continue to function with such a pitiful headcount.

She was about to ascend the stairs to her office when she spotted old Mr Cavendish. When he saw her, his face lit up. Politely, he yanked the cap off his head.

"Mrs Stockwell. I heard you were here today. Might I say we all appreciate your visit very much? There's nothing to worry about. We briefed the young men on what to expect. All of them want to offer their full support. Let us know when you're ready for the tour, and we'll highlight the issues we've encountered of late."

"Thank you, Mr Cavendish."

A gaggle of curious faces began gathering around them, like schoolboys around a pair fighting.

"Where is your son? I have not seen him so far. What time does he plan to arrive?"

"Oh, he's here already."

"Forgive me. I was wrong to assume the worst. How rude."

"Ah, it's nothing. Don't you worry. You wouldn't be the first to think he was pulling a fast one," he chuckled. "No, he's over in the warehouse, working with old Finnegan to organise some of the raw materials. They are arranging everything for your inspection right now. My Jon might never have held down a permanent job, but he makes up for it with dedication and enthusiasm. If he's not doing a task you have set him, I guarantee he'll be pitching in wherever the lads say he's needed."

"Wonderful. I am glad to hear it."

She was disappointed in herself. Richard had mentioned the men's loyalty for years. It was James who had accused them of being bone idle. It was another sign of her brother's ineptitude. She decided to keep any derogatory opinions to herself in future. For the rest of the day, Georgina didn't spot a single slack-jawed worker amongst the brewers.

The storehouse and loading dock were separated by a small passage towards the back of the brewery. She had no idea which door she needed, so she picked the left one at random.

She had made a mistake, but it turned out to be a fortuitous one. The door led to a first-floor landing. Below was something that smelled like it was fermenting. Once Georgina realised her wrong turn, she could have easily spun on her heels and gone back to the passageway, but she was eager to learn more about her new environment. With no one around, she carefully descended the narrow wooden steps, with one hand holding onto a slimy wet metal railing, the other lifting her skirts, so she didn't trip and break her neck.

The place was dank and gloomy. She couldn't see much, but she could feel the dirt floor beneath her feet to tell her she'd reached the bottom of the steps. Very little light made it down to the floor area, just a few thin shards of light that worked their way through the cracks and gaps in the building and a few flickering lanterns. She showed no signs of fear, finding the smell of damp earth and fermenting grain strangely natural, like she was walking through woodland. The cold clamminess of the air didn't trouble her either. Even though she was in the centre of a bustling brewery in London's East End, she felt she could relax and enjoy the tranquillity of the place. Undoubtedly, it helped not to have an army of workers staring at her.

Suddenly, there was more lantern light. As it swayed, it was accompanied by footsteps echoing down the stairs. Georgina turned around.

"Mr Cavendish!"

"I could have sworn we'd agreed I'd be called Jon?" he teased.

His natural and relaxed demeanour was a delight. She thanked her lucky stars for the darkness, so he couldn't see the flush rising on her cheeks.

"I do apologise—Jon. Gosh, saying that feels odd and quite normal. All morning I've been referring to you as Jon in my thoughts, yet your name, Mr Cavendish, comes out when I address you in person."

"I imagine it is difficult to abandon such polite protocols. They have been drilled into you since birth. No doubt I'll slip up and call you Mrs Stockwell at some point."

With the small talk over with, silence surrounded them for a few seconds until Jon finally spoke.

"I see you've found the crypt—"

"Really! Is that its name?" she gulped.

"I'm pulling your leg. It's the cellar."

"When I first arrived, I was trying to locate the warehouse area. Your father said I would find you there with—Fergus?"

"Finnegan"

"Yes, that's the chap. Well, when I saw these steps leading down, I had to come to investigate."

"Is that right? So, you don't have a fear of the dark, then?"

"Not unless there is good reason to be afraid."

"You might be a bit perturbed about some of the dark alleyways by my neck of the woods in Whitechapel."

"No, I am sure those are places one wouldn't want to be at night. Whereas a cellar? My cellar? In a bustling brewery? Well, all that might be here are rats and the odd ghost."

"You're a brave soul, ain't ya."

She laughed off the compliment and smiled.

"Nevertheless, I feel guilty about wandering about alone. I have no business being here. It feels like I am covertly checking up on the men, which I promise you I wasn't."

Her explanation drew nothing but a feeble shrug from Jon.

"I feel like a naughty child caught wagging off school. You have more right to be here than me."

"Nowt to feel guilty about. You said you would run the business. Why wouldn't you want to explore it?"

"That's as may be, but in terms of time served here, the men have far more of a claim on the place than I do. They know every nook and cranny. How the place lives and breathes. This reminds me what a fish I am out of water."

"Well, it's bound to feel strange. What with you being a woman and all, too. Spend enough time here, and I am sure it will feel like a second home— like you belong here."

Jon's face glowed in the lantern light. His expression exuded confidence.

"You seem so certain. I wish I could be convinced too."

He gave a charming smirk.

"Well, that's the trick to it, innit, missus. Just act like you're confident til you are. None of the lads are going to test your mettle. They wouldn't dare after you fired them all on a whim," he joked before becoming a little more serious. "If you act like you know what you're doing often enough, you might just convince yourself that you know something for real."

"Is that so?

"That strategy's worked well for me so far in me twenty-odd years."

"I shall take that phrase to heart and live by it."

She took a look at the vast hall with its neat rows of oak barrels.

"I think I ought to find out what's in here, shouldn't I. What exactly is held in all those barrels, and for how long?"

"You and me both, remember. I only worked down the docks for Stockwell's. I only know what a good pint tastes like at the moment, and I gleaned a few bits and bobs off me dad. Still, working with old Finnegan at the warehouse today has been what you might call 'illuminating'. It's helped me understand what I'll be flogging."

He chuckled as he lifted the lantern to his face.

"I tell you what. Why don't I just tag along and learn what Mr Finnegan is showing you?"

"An excellent suggestion. Shall we?"

They climbed the stairs together, with Jon holding the lantern high so they could both keep their footing. The ominous creaking of the ancient stairs was amplified by their weight.

"Perhaps, we should go one by one next time?"

"Agreed."

He smiled at her in a way that made her heart do a little unexpected flip. She hoped his charm worked as well on men as it did on her.

Old Finnegan was a slender, wiry man. He looked tough and street-wise, the sort of bloke who would lurk in a dark alley, staring at the glint of a blade, prepared to defend himself to the death when threatened. The intensity of his gaze pierced her just as easily as a knife through her soft flesh.

As time passed, keeping to her promise to avoid assuming the worst in people, she decided she had judged him harshly too. Like the rest of her workforce, Finnegan might be uneducated in the formal sense, but he was by no means stupid. An enthusiastic fellow who took pride in his profession, he walked her through the intricacies of his work. Before moving on to the next aspect, he would ask her probing questions to ensure she knew everything. She liked his honest and direct manner.

He made a small, decisive slit in a sack so she could inspect the contents. She wasn't sure what was in it.

"Here, missus, you take 'em out and sniff 'em like this."

He demonstrated slowly, concealing the contents in his hand.

"Go on."

When Georgina touched the product, she realised it was dried hop blossoms.

He showed her how to sample the product again. She lifted the crispy brown leaves to her nose and sniffed deeply. The bitter odour was strong and memorable.

"Well, it's obviously hops, Mr Finnegan, but I suspect you expect more from me."

"Indeed, I do Mrs Stockwell. Can you hazard a guess as to the quality of the product?"

"Not really. I am fairly sure it's not from the consignment that Mr Duffield bought that had fallen in the docks."

"Correct. So, what is its provenance then?"

"Provenance?"

"Where did it come from? Hereford? Kent? Germany?"

"Kent?"

"Sadly, an incorrect guess. Hereford. It's acceptable but not as good as when Mr Richard was in charge."

"Germany, then? Everyone knows German beer is good quality."

"You might think that, but connoisseurs say that Kent produces the best hops in the world. And it's right on our doorstep. Did you know that your brother only used hops from the 'Garden of England'?

"No, I didn't. But what makes it so special? Hops smell like hops to me."

"The climate in Kent is ideal for cultivation. I don't need to sniff this to know it's not from Kent."

"You know quite a bit about hops."

"Aye, that's true. Your brother would buy all sorts of hops, looking to save a bob or two per tonne. I got to see a lot in my time. But I knew a lot before that."

Confidently, Finnegan straightened up, put his hops sample in a bucket and brushed his hands together to remove the dust.

"My grandpa farmed hops. I used to help him as a young lad. Hours and hours we spent together during harvest time. After he died, my pa uprooted our family and moved us to London. He might have taken me out of the countryside, but he couldn't take the countryside out of me."

"I can tell. Your knowledge is positively encyclopaedic, Mr Finnegan," said Georgina.

"Now, get your hooter round some of this," he said, slicing at another sack.

Georgina leaned in towards his hand and sniffed. Georgina winced.

"Now, do they have a musty odour to you?"

The eyes of Finnegan were on her. She forced herself to take another deep breath while leaning over the bag.

"Yes, there is more than a hint of it in there. What causes it to form that mustiness? It wasn't some of that stock that fell in the water, was it? If it was, I am so sorry my brother purchased it."

"No, we had to use that when we had no other hops on hand," Finnegan snarled through his teeth.

"Oh!" said Georgina in shock.

Finnegan bent his head and cast a sneaking look toward Jon.

"As I explained to this young man, missus, the damp's coming into the storage room over there," he said as he angled his finger toward the room's far side.

"How long have we had a leak? Weeks—Months—?"

Finnegan shook his head.

"It pains me to say this, Mrs Stockwell, but I informed Mr Duffield about this problem two years ago. He had a few planks nailed over the ingress points, but wood isn't very effective at preventing moisture build-up. For one thing, when it's untreated, it's absorbent. Secondly, wet wood rots. The wood Mr Duffield put up last spring has already perished. He never bothered putting up anymore. He ignored me when I pressed him on it."

It was evident that James's misdemeanour upset Mr Finnegan greatly. Worse, Georgina suspected the man wasn't sure she would take his complaint seriously. Why should he? Duffield had ignored him before—apart from making a repair so poor, so patronising, it was more irritating than being ignored entirely.

"So, where is the water coming in, Mr Finnegan?"

Finnegan's penetrating gaze broadened just a little. He nodded into the distance.

"Follow me. You'd better come too, Jon."

He led the trio over to some empty barrels on a deep shelf.

You'll find it hidden underneath these. But unless you go on all fours, you won't see well.

"Then, gentlemen, on all fours, I shall go."

She loosened the bottom few buttons on her waistcoat, lifted her skirt up to the top of her boots, then stopped, knowing she would need to lift it higher to kneel down properly, but hesitating. Jon began to giggle.

"Why do you find my wanting to investigate the matter fully so amusing, Mr Cavendish?"

"Well, the cuffs on your nice white blouse will be caked in mud soon, never mind your knees."

"I'll have you know this shirt was a gift from my mother. I hated it from the moment I got it. That is exactly why I wore it today. If it got sullied or torn, then that was all to the good. I would finally be rid of it."

Once she had arranged her cumbersome clothing, she went on her hands and knees, and began to peer among the barrels. As she eased in, she was sure Jon and Mr Finnegan saw her upturned rear wiggle at them, but she didn't give a hoot. Her primary goals were knowledge and experience. Vanity and decorum were not a concern. Convincing Mr Finnegan she was troubled by his complaint was. Richard had never been afraid to roll up his sleeves and muck in with his men. Now, it was her turn to do the same.

Finnegan was spot-on. Light was streaming through the brickwork. It looked like the wood had rotted away completely. The wet had got into the mortar, and it looked like the stonework was deteriorating too.

"Well, that will need to be mended properly," she advised as she crawled back out.

She got to her feet and turned to look directly at Mr Finnegan.

"I promise this will be fixed to your satisfaction. Please allow me some time."

"It's not as easy as it looks. That's a perimeter wall. It backs onto another fella's land. And you won't be surprised to hear him and Mr Duffield had a bit of a falling out. You'll have to smooth him over first to get access."

"I give you my word that it will be resolved this week. As you can imagine, the list of the men's grievances is long and complicated. Everyone wants their problem dealt with first. But I won't forget about this. Thank you for explaining the issue so well."

"I believe you, missus.—By the way, you're welcome."

It seemed strange, but Georgina felt an intense warm glow from Finnegan's praise.

After her first in-depth and productive introduction to an employee, she was keen to do more. She commented to one man that she thought seeing all James's failures would be soul-destroying, but they had ended up being quite the opposite and galvanising her into action. It strengthened her drive to outshine him immeasurably. It was time to get the brewery back to its former glory when the Stockwells ran it.

The men were looking at her with such expectation that she couldn't bear to disappoint them. The rebirth had to happen. After getting to know them and giving them a chance to contribute some fantastic ideas, Georgina realised that these men loved the company just as much as she did. They took great delight in their work, instantly making Georgina feel the same way. All she had to do now was not let them down.

During the rest of her trip, Jon never left her side. He sensed something about his presence that made Georgina happy, not just because he was absorbing important information.

After finishing the last tours, Georgina returned to the office to do some paperwork. When she entered, the clerk, a mild-mannered man called Bridges, emerged from behind a stack of files to greet her. She took her seat at Richard's old desk. It was a bittersweet moment, but one that she would treasure for the rest of her life.

The desk looked a total mess. Richard used to pride himself in leaving it clear of any paperwork at the end of the day. Now, his beautiful mahogany desk was littered with files.

She found a collection of empty port bottles in the drawers that belonged to her brother. She took them out and threw them in a sack in a temper. Their clanking interrupted Bridges from his work, but he didn't mind. It was another reminder of James that he was glad to see the back of.

Soon, Georgina had it looking spik and span again. The desk itself was well over a century old. She ran her fingers along the smooth wood. Richard told her how his great-great-grandfather had imported it from India. He'd kept it in the first family bottle shop in the days before the family had the money to build their own brewery. She spotted a dotted ring of red, carelessly left by a bottle of port over in the far corner of the desk. Georgina felt it was a microcosm of his impact on the company as a whole, systematically ruining everything that was good about it with his selfish carelessness.

Although the stain wasn't done by her hand, she felt responsible. She had turned a blind eye to James's poor performance and told herself it was outside her remit. Now she felt responsible for the damage done to the business, the men, and the product the family used to pride itself on.

"Damn you, James", she muttered as she scrubbed at the mark, although it refused to fade.

The gloomy office had no sign of Richard anymore. He lived a simple life and wasn't the sort of man to stamp his mark on a place. The office was filled with heirlooms, portraits and personal touches from his ancestors, who had all contributed to its furnishing, but there was nothing of Richard's.

For many years, he worked his standard schedule of ten hours daily, except Sundays, but he never forced his opinions or views on the building. It was similar to how her husband had managed the company. It chugged like an impressive steam engine, yet no one stopped admiring its beauty. It was just there, doing its thing. She stopped scrubbing. Her last thought felt cold, cruel even. She hoped he wasn't listening to her thoughts in heaven. She wasn't saying her husband didn't matter, more that he was the invisible glue that held things together and made them work well. Perhaps it was a superstition, but she just couldn't seem to shake the image of him from her mind here, in the place where he had spent so much of his short life. She loved him deeply then, and she loved him still. The last thing she wanted to do was anger him in a place he held so close to his heart.

Perhaps if they had borne a son, he would have been the one to lay the foundations on that new path the company needed to take en route to a better future. Richard had craved a son more than anything else, apart from his wife and the family business. Sadly, they were blessed with neither a boy nor a girl during their union. Like the navvies laying new train tracks across countries and continents, Georgina would have to support the new course for the brewery. It was a tough assignment but also a thrilling one.

Only now did she realise how lucky she was to have found Jon Cavendish. The men knew how to fix the fabric of the building and how it operated, but they were out of their depth when it came to the world outside the brewery's perimeter. Jon Cavendish was a man of the world, albeit based in London. He understood people, and that's the thing she needed most of all to win over the hearts and minds of those who had been let down beyond the brewery. She strongly felt that he would play a significant role in assisting her to resurrect the business. Or, perhaps, had the hand of fate drawn them together for some strange, higher purpose? It was turning into a strong feeling she couldn't deny. A curious sense of destiny. She dismissed the thought, telling herself off for becoming superstitious again.

She wandered across the office to the big window and looked down at the men working. Over in one corner, she watched Jon observe as his pa put some barley in one of the copper stills. Although Georgina was far away, she could see him paying attention to his father's every word, asking him questions and copying his father's actions.

He cut a handsome figure, Jon Cavendish. Dark curls framed a rugged face and intelligent, sparkling eyes. She presumed all the girls of Whitechapel must be mad for him. Why wouldn't they be?

Her head snapped away from the window. It was the second unfortunate thought that day that Georgina had succumbed to about the man, an employee. Had she no shame?

Once again, she hoped Richard, high up with the angels, had not been able to hear that thought.

11

THE STEEP
LEARNING CURVE

Some of the best times in Georgina's life were during her first few days at Stockwell & Sons. She dived headfirst into the production process, realising that she greatly loved her work. It was hard graft but rewarding, giving her a sense of accomplishment and fulfilment at the day's end. A feeling that was time well spent.

In their alone time after dinner, Richard used to share the love of his brewery work with her. But there was always the implication that she should not pursue a career in the family business. Both the Stockwell and the Duffield families decided Georgina should do like all respectable wives of her era and devote some of her spare time to helping others. Philanthropic and charitable work would be her only outlets for stimulus outside the family home. Although Georgina was sympathetic to the idea of helping the deserving poor, she found that the volunteer work she was assigned to was cold and uninspiring. It seemed more like an opportunity to look down on the lower classes rather than raise them up.

After her brief taste, Georgina was enamoured with the brewery's energetic nerve centre. The brewery she owned. So, when someone came along to put a spanner in the works of her newfound sense of purpose, she was heartbroken. She was not surprised, though. Her family seemed to thrive on spite and selfishness. Georgina forging her own path in life was definitely frowned upon.

She loved her new profession so much that even after a full day of work, Georgina spent a good portion observing the repairs, even helping when the men let her. She'd come home through the chill autumn air, warmed by the glow of the gas lamps, with a keen desire for nothing more than a bowl of hot soup and her cosy bed. That was soon to end when on her return one evening, she was handed a letter by Mr McKay. She didn't want to open the correspondence. If she didn't open it, her life could trundle along merrily on its happy new route. But, sadly, that was not an option.

"No postmark or sender's address?"

"No, ma'am."

"It looks like Duffield family stationery?"

"I agree, ma'am. And possibly your mother's handwriting."

"Thank you, Mr McKay. I was trying not to notice that."

McKay looked regretfully at the mistress of the house.

"I always find it's better to face up to problems as soon as they occur."

Georgina ripped the envelope open and skimmed through the letter.

"Mrs Duffield arrived here just before noon. I advised her you weren't at home, and she went directly to the library. She insisted you received the letter as soon as you got home." He looked apologetically at Georgina. "I'm sorry, ma'am. I understand how your mother sometimes distresses you."

"I am a grown woman, a widow and now a business owner, Mr McKay. And yet still, my mother insists on treating me like a little girl."

Georgina sensed she was starting to wallow, to pity herself, and that was something that her new tough business persona would never do.

Georgina Stockwell, the businesswoman, decided she would no longer waste time wallowing.

"Forgive me, Mr McKay. I won't be much company. I think I shall retire for the evening."

"There's nothing to forgive, ma'am. Shall I send Sarah to your room with a hot chocolate?"

"Brandy, I think tonight, Mr McKay. Oh, and can you see about getting in a selection of ales. Youngs, Fullers, maybe? If I am making ale, I think I should start to partake in some occasionally. For research purposes only, of course," she said with a twinkle.

"Of course, ma'am. Research."

Even as he nodded thoughtfully, the elderly butler smiled a little.

"Oh, and Mr McKay—"

"Ma'am?"

"Thanks for being so dependable."

"My pleasure, ma'am."

He put away her coat, thinking about the note in his mistress's hand. It would not be then that he discovered the nature of its contents.

Mrs Stockwell breezed off to the living room and shut the door behind her. Alone, she took off the mask of quiet confidence and slumped onto an armchair, seemingly defeated, before reading a single word. She opened the letter with trembling hands, unfolded the paper inside, and started to read.

Her worst fears had been realised.

Georgina,

I won't sugar-coat this. I am staggered to hear from your brother James that he has been ousted from the business by you and Mr Bainbridge acting in cahoots! Further, it has been relayed to me that you've been observed not only visiting, but working at the brewery daily for the past week. At first, I thought it was idle tittle-tattle, but James informed me the information was accurate.

May I remind you, Georgina, that you are a young lady from a respectable family? A lady of your social standing has no place running a business, much less one in Whitechapel that manufactures alcoholic beverages!

Your father and I are appalled and ashamed by your carry-on. We want you to stop immediately. I understand why you don't wish to put your brother

*back in charge of the business. I shall instruct Mr
Bainbridge to start looking for a suitable
replacement.*

Your ever-loving mother.

Georgina was fuming. She stood up and briskly paced from
one side of the room to the other, muttering as she clutched
onto the fluttering letter. The young woman was tired of her
mother assuming she could meddle in her life. Thankfully,
she could finally stand up to her. Her claim to the company
was secure now she had settled the debts, and Mr Bainbridge
knew she wanted to assume leadership. As far as Georgina
was concerned, her mother's letter was another bump in the
road she would have to drive over.

Georgina would not be deterred by her mother's letter or her
wishes. No, she would carry on as she was. In the meantime,
she would do her utmost to dodge her mother. Even if Mrs
Duffield couldn't legally intervene, it wouldn't stop her
from trying to strong-arm her daughter or Mr Bainbridge
with her sharp tongue. She excelled at grinding people down
until they gave in to her wishes, just to make the verbal
assault stop. Over the years, Georgina learned she was not
the only one who thought confrontation with Mrs Ruth
Duffield was something to be avoided at all costs.

12

THE LITMUS TEST

Jon's big day finally arrived. This was the first time he had to prove himself. Georgina had written to ask the largest and angriest of her former suppliers to meet with Stockwell & Sons, and they had accepted. Before the incompetent Duffield ruined the relationship, the brewery depended heavily on this wholesaler to get the best quality product to the warehouse from a collection of leading Kent growers.

Jon was apprehensive. Even though he knew he could 'convince a rabbit to give up its ears on the hop', he worried he wouldn't be able to perform as well when prompted. The stakes were a lot higher. If he lost a day's work, he would go hungry. Mess this negotiation up, and he might lose his job. Everyone might lose their jobs if Georgina couldn't source better ingredients. He was terrified to fluff the deal because of the nerves that accompanied the pressure he was under.

His dad was disappointed that Jon didn't prepare the night before. He'd offered to role play with his son, but no, he wasn't interested. He gave Jon a pen and paper to jot down notes. He refused. Finally, he reminded his boy about how much faith Georgina had put in him and that he was duty-bound to do his best.

"You might be comfortable with letting this meeting slide. I am not. Now, sit up straight. I'll be the supplier."

"What's the point, pa? We've never negotiated a commercial contract before? How will you know what the chap's going to say?"

"If you think he would say something specific, you can practise responding to it."

"Cor. There's no way of knowing. We could go till morning."

David threw his hands in the air. "Heaven help me, Jon! Tomorrow will be one of the most important days of your life, and you're sitting here like a lemon, doing nothing."

Jon ran his fingers through his curly black hair to soothe his aching brain.

"You're going to work me into a right tizzy with this. Please, just stop going on about it. I was hired because Georgina thinks I pass muster. She's only ever seen me speak off the cuff. If I let my emotions get the best of me and try and engineer the encounter to go my way, I'll end up saying stupid things. Just leave me alone, will you?"

"Fine. I'm going to bed," said his father before stomping off.

Jon wracked his brain like a chess player trying to contemplate all the moves and all the likely responses in a game. It was useless. There were too many parameters. No, there was nothing to do except get a good night's sleep. He was relieved that he felt drowsy as soon as his head hit his thin pillow, and it wouldn't be one of those nights where he blinked, staring into the blackness, trying to will himself to sleep and failing.

He got up an hour earlier than usual and meticulously prepared for the day. His shirt was freshly washed and ironed thanks to Rachel. Jon carefully buttoned it up, popped on his tie and then combed his unruly hair into some sort of style. He looked in the mirror. He decided he looked convincing as a white-collar businessman, not a blue-collar dock hand.

He thought of Georgina, wondering if she was worrying too. Perhaps she, too, was pondering how it might turn out as she brushed her hair.

He soon pulled himself up by his bootstraps. What was he doing considering everything that could go wrong? Foolishly tempting fate like that? He corrected himself, saying he should think about everything that could go right.

Jon left his family's lodgings long before his father was awake, keen to avoid another grilling about what he should and shouldn't be doing. He strolled the short distance to the brewery while thinking happy thoughts. He popped to Mr Horowitz's bakery at the junction of Dean Street and Brooks Road to treat himself to a gloriously sticky iced bun. It was extravagant, but it felt as good a day as any to indulge. His first wage packet was due on the morrow. If there was ever a good time to splurge, this was it.

The sweet, sticky treat bread relaxed him just enough. By the time he arrived at the brewery, he was in his usual jovial mood. He stepped through the gates and noticed the gentle glow of the office lights illuminating the brewery floor.

Georgina was focused on the papers on her desk until she heard a gentle knock at the open door. Her beautiful brown eyes spun across to meet Jon's. When he saw that she was pleased to see him, it helped him relax more.

"You're early," she said.

"And you."

"Well, I ought to be, really. It is my business," Georgina chuckled.

Jon folded his arms across his chest and leaned on the door.

"I probably shouldn't say, but it seems to me that the prosperity or failure of this establishment feels just as much my concern as yours."

"I am sorry for burdening you like that."

"Ah, don't worry. I love a good challenge, me. It makes me feel alive."

"Well, that's good, Jon, because you're going to face many challenges. Mr Bainbridge has told me about the past year's sales data. It's not pleasant reading."

"But you knew there were problems when you agreed to take this place on. What's changed?"

"I hadn't appreciated their true scale—nor the rate at which they are worsening."

He'd entered the office and was observing her from a distance.

"Come on, then. What are these trends you've seen?"

The question was met with a shake of her head.

"Well, last year, our best performing ale sold less than the worst performing line when Richard was in charge. Twenty per cent less."

"Ouch!"

"No matter what I do here to modernise the facilities, if people don't trust us, and hate our products, then what's the point in carrying on? And what's worse is that now I am more dependent on your linguistic wizardry than ever at the start of this mess. I feel like everything that matters to me will sink without trace, and it's all my fault."

Jon scowled at her with pinched brows.

"What time did you get here? It looks like quite a while ago?

"Possibly."

"Come on, tell me."

"Five?" She said hesitantly.

Outside, St Matthew's church bells rang out six times.

"Four?" she said with a weak smile.

When he saw her face flush with shame, he changed tack.

"Have you had breakfast?"

She remained tight-lipped. As time passed, the pink shade became more intense.

"I didn't want to wake up the cook. You see, Mrs Hargrove is such a dedicated soul. She would have been crushed if she had not anticipated my early departure. I thought it easier to sneak out and let Mr McKay tell her a little white lie."

Jon laughed as he pictured the chaotic scene back in Mayfair.

"Well then, let us get you some food."

"As in? What—out there?"

"Yes, out there."

"In Whitechapel?"

"Yes. When did you wake up again, Georgina? You seem very disorientated?" he teased. "What are you so scared of? I will come with you, you know?"

"I've never done much exploring of the great outdoors by myself. Normally never further than it takes to get to my carriage from the entrance of whatever place I am visiting."

"Don't fret; I'll take care of you."

She stayed rooted to the spot when he cocked his head towards the exit.

"C'mon. You must eat."

"Will you shut up about food if I go?"

"Of course."

"Fine. Well, come on then, Mr Cavendish. Chop chop."

Together, they emerged into the busy streets of Whitechapel and made their way to Commercial road. Jon could see that Georgina's shy demeanour was caused by her apprehension. All around her were strange things, some loud, some filthy. That applied to the throngs of people she saw too. No matter how timid she looked, she never looked condescending, which he found a lovely, heartwarming trait.

He leaned down towards her ear and spoke just loud enough to be heard above the crowd.

"What do you fancy, then?"

"What do you recommend?"

"Probably best not to go for these first."

They walked by a toothless woman selling boiled pig trotters of questionable freshness, all served with a scowl.

"Unless the butcher lets you give stuff a good sniff before buying it, I wouldn't recommend any meat around here."

He led her away from the pig lady and towards a man selling plum pudding that looked much more appealing.

"I've never tried plum pudding, Jon."

"Never? Have you been living under a stone, Georgina? Me mother used to make it every Sunday—when we could afford it. My poor sister Rachel tries so hard to make it just like ma used to, but somehow, it doesn't quite hit the same spot.

She's so disappointed. I tell her it's lovely, but she doesn't believe me. I mean, it is lovely. It's just not—"

"—the same," said Georgina with a comforting smile. "Richard used to make the best cups of tea."

"Ready to try some?" Jon said, keen to lighten the tone of their conversation.

"Now, apart from my ma's and Rachel's, this is the best plum pudding this side of the Savoy."

While she nibbled, Jon watched her expression, looking for clues about her opinion.

"I bet it's not as nice as the Christmas pudding you're used to?" said Jon, still looking for her reaction.

There was a trace of embarrassment in her grin.

"It's actually perfect for 9 a.m. I'm impressed," she confessed, taking bigger and bigger bites.

"Anything tastes nice when you're hungry," he said, a little dismissively. He picked up on his mistake and blurted out, "I'm sorry. What happened to my manners?"

"They went to the same place mine went to. I didn't offer you any, did I!" chuckled Georgina as she popped the last piece of pudding into her mouth.

"I think plum pudding was more appropriate than pickled whelks or jellied eels. That stuff can make you have a funny turn if you're not used to it. I am guessing you don't want to be bothered with an upset stomach today?"

"Are you anxious about today, Jon ? Mine keeps doing little somersaults when I think about the meeting. I am telling myself it is excitement—"

"Are you kidding? I'm excited. It's my time to shine!" he lied. "I remind myself that he's just another man like me. No better, no worse. And there are so many ways we could work with him. And even if everything went completely wrong, he's not the only fella peddling decent hops around here."

"I know, but I can't help feeling like this is a pivotal point. If I can't undo the damage James did to the relationship by offering the carrot that is a significant regular order on the end of my stick, then what hope do I have that I can undo the rest?"

He turned to face her and held her by her shoulders. He gazed into her eyes.

"Georgina, listen to me. There is always more than one way to get something done. If you hit a snag, it's rarely fatal, is it?"

"Are you trying to be flippant, or is it happening by mistake?"

"Suppose you don't win over this seller. In fact, things go so badly that you don't win over any hops sellers. Mr Duffield's reputation is so toxic that no hops seller in Europe will supply their goods to you. You'll still be fine."

"Have you taken leave of your senses, Jon?"

"No, but you might have. If you have no hops, you must find something else to brew."

"But we're a brewery, Jon !"

"Well, perhaps you need to have another chat with your master brewers. Not all ale recipes require hops."

"Really?" she asked, looking back at him bemused and delighted.

"Yes, really."

"I hope that conviction of yours will come through in our meeting today. The way you speak makes me almost believe I can do it."

"You can do it. I know you can," he said gently, as he gave her shoulders a soft, reassuring shake.

She patted the back of his right hand with hers. The warmth of the touch travelled up his arm and set his heart alight. At that moment, he was aware he was still holding onto her, still staring into her eyes. He reluctantly let her go.

"I suppose we'd better get back," he advised. "The first shift will arrive in five minutes, and if they come and spot an unlocked and empty office, they'll think James has kidnapped you."

Georgina gave a nervous laugh.

"Don't tempt fate," she said.

13

'I CAN ONLY APOLOGISE FOR MY BROTHER'

Georgina watched the clock in the office ticking. The distraction was welcome. By now, she was a nervous wreck on the sides. Somehow, she still had enough control for it not to show. Jon Cavendish, on the other hand, seemed perfectly relaxed. She had no idea what to anticipate about the hops distributor coming to see them. All she knew was his name. Mr Tate of Lambeth. After her brother's shabby treatment of the man, she prepared herself for a severe reprimand.

She heard the footsteps of Mr Bridges followed by another set. Her mouth went dry. The steps stopped, and there was a gentle knock at the door.

"Mr Tate is here to see you, ma'am."

"Wonderful, Mr Bridges. Thank you. Please, Mr Tate, do come in."

The man was nothing like the person Georgina had imagined. She had pictured a big brute of a man. Hard-nosed. Pushy. Angry. But Mr Tate did not cut the figure of an imposing leader of a powerful industrialist family. He'd more in common with Mr Bainbridge than a bully. He was polite and unassuming. He seemed unremarkable, stood there with middling height, middling build, middling demeanour. Despite that, Georgina still felt on edge. She put it down to one of the perils of having a conscience.

Although most of his appearance was bland, the dismissive expression on his face was inescapable. She and Jon could tell the abysmal treatment his company had received at the hands of James was still bothering him. As Mr Tate sat down and opened his briefcase, Georgina gave a concerned sideways glance to Jon. He gave a little encouraging smile and nod, but still, she felt like she was like a warrior going into her battle, unarmed and unprepared.

"Thank you for inviting me to come and see you, Mrs Stockwell. I must confess I was rather surprised to hear from you. Given the circumstances."

"I think you are referring to my brother. I can assure you he has left the business, and I am the new legal owner of Stockwell & Sons, thanks to the work done by Mr Bainbridge, whom you might have met?"

"Oh, I've met him. He was here when your brother was spinning me his yarns and stitching me up. James Duffield was a charlatan. I wish I had realised sooner."

"I can assure you—"

Tate cut her off, impatient to finally detail all the transgressions that had caused so much trouble.

"Did you know he swindled me out of hundreds of pounds?"

His piercing gaze made Georgina gulp with guilt.

"Hundreds."

His finger traced down a sheet of paper.

"Yes. Here is the evidence to back up my claim," he said as he turned the sheet around and pushed it under her nose.

"And there's more."

His fingers danced over another column of figures, tapping in several places.

"Please accept my apologies, Mr Tate."

"With respect, Mrs Stockwell, apologies are lovely, but they won't fix your account with us."

Georgina wasn't sure how to respond. She decided listening earnestly was her best option. Jon said nothing. She glanced at him, but when all he did was shrug, she bit the inside of her cheek hard in an attempt to keep her composure. She often did it when faced with her angry mother when she was on the warpath about some transgression or other.

"The stories he told me were as magnificent as they were deceitful. He explained to me once that the sale of his ale hadn't gone as well as he'd hoped, and thus, he couldn't settle his debt for a few months. Then I read in the paper a bit later that he's bought himself a share of a thoroughbred racehorse with some of the fellows from his exclusive

Gentlemen's club. I have no idea what a racehorse costs, but I do know it costs two hundred guineas a year to be a member of that club, which was roughly what he owed me!"

"That must have been awful to discover. I can only apol—"

Now he'd sniffed blood, Mr Tate had no intention of holding back.

"—and then the next time he ran out of funds, he told me I'd sold him poor-quality hops. He reckoned the poor harvest that year was the reason for it. Yes, it had been a cruel summer, but it had only affected the quantity, not the quality of what we supplied him. He tried to pull a fast one saying it had affected the taste of his brew, and that was why it hadn't sold. He had the cheek to blame me for those losses of his making, said I shared responsibility for the problem and 'I could whistle' if I expected to be paid in full for 'subpar materials'. He wanted to pay twenty per cent of the true value, the rogue! What could I do? He'd already had the stock."

Tate detailed several more grievances, all completely valid. Georgina wanted to run and hide. In the end, she confessed to feeling the man's pain more acutely than he might have imagined.

Jon stayed at a discreet distance behind Georgina during the meeting, observing Mr Tate closely. Georgina was praying he would step in with some of his wise words and save her from the savaging. Finally, he did.

"Forgive me for interrupting, Mr Tate. Jonathan Cavendish, business advisor to Mrs Stockwell. How do you do?"

Jon gave the man a firm handshake and looked at him solemnly.

"I have a quick question. I am keen to understand more about this situation. This might sound strange, and I apologise in advance if I offend you. The last thing I want to do is question your expertise. It's just I'm curious. Why did you keep doing business with Mr Duffield after discovering his dishonesty? Why not just refuse to trade with him?"

Mr Tate's face hardened. Georgina wasn't sure if it was defeat, regret or anger.

"With the benefit of hindsight, I can see my mistake. This painful experience taught me that emotion has no place in the commercial world. The answer is simple. It was loyalty. You may or may not be aware, but Tate and Blackwell have been doing business with Stockwell & Sons for over a century. Our two businesses were formed around the same time. I have wonderful memories of Mr Richard, but before that, I can remember my grandpa always dealing with his grandpa. It was such a treat to visit here when I was a wee boy. The two old men were more like brothers than colleagues. Always looking out for each other. Working together, profiting together."

Georgina's gaze sank to her lap. Once again, she felt betrayed by James. How dare he exploit such a longstanding and treasured professional connection!

"I gave him the benefit of the doubt. He came from a respectable family, as does Mrs Stockwell, so I had no reason to suspect he would renege on the values of the industrialist elite into which he was born. His father was a successful entrepreneur in his own right. I expected James to uphold the same values. I knew he was new to managing a brewery, so I expected a few hiccups at the start of his tenure, but I fear I gave him the benefit of the doubt a few times too many. Then it was too late, of course. James seemed to enjoy fleecing us all the more when he knew he could 'get away with it'. It took me longer than I might like to get wise to his antics. But I refused to supply hops to him anymore when I did."

"I see, Mr Tate. That makes perfect sense now. The good news is Mrs Stockwell does uphold the business values you respect. She wants to follow in Mr Stockwell's footsteps, not her brothers."

"That's all well and good, Mr Cavendish, but that alone won't fix the gaping hole in my balance sheet. Now, I'm not a greedy man, but we did suffer. With the poor harvest and the parlous state of the nation's finances, the price of beer went up. Folks weren't drinking as much as they used to. Demand collapsed. My costs rose. My revenue tumbled. Things got so bad after Mr Duffield ripped us off that I had to pay my employees out of my own pocket for two months."

Georgina didn't need Jon's help to know what to say.

"That is a disgrace, Mr Tate. There is absolutely no doubt in my mind that the Stockwell's debts need to be repaid in full. Would you please excuse me briefly while I discuss this delicate matter privately with Mr Cavendish?"

Mr Tate gave a begrudging nod.

"Perhaps I can ask Mr Bridges to fetch you a cup of tea?"

"No, thank you," said Tate as he got out of his chair and walked to the big window.

He saw the two of them walk to the bottom of the stairs, deep in discussion.

"Jon, I simply don't have the funds to pay him the balance right now. Not if I want to fix the rusting stills, the warehouse's crumbling brickwork and everything else! What are we going to do?" said Georgina, trying not to whimper.

Jon nodded and nibbled thoughtfully on his lower lip. He appeared unruffled and confident, unlike Georgina, whose mounting sense of hopelessness was killing her. The only thing that kept her going was remembering he had been her source of strength in the past, and he needed to do something miraculous once more.

"Of course! That's it!" he said at last.

"What's it?"

"I can't say. I need to flesh it all out in the moment, else I might muck up the real negotiation. Can I ask one thing? How much money do you have on hand for raw materials?"

"Three months. At best, why?"

"Perfect."

"What's perfect?" she said as their eyes locked.

He put his fingers to his lips.

"Whatever you're thinking, Jon Cavendish, just don't put me in more debt."

"Can't promise, luv. Let's see how it pans out," he said with a cheeky wink.

Georgina felt sick as the two of them went back upstairs. Her knees threatened to buckle, and her ivory skin looked paler than ever.

Mr Tate was back at the desk, his fingers toying with a gold paperweight more exquisite than anything he had seen before. Hearing their return, he quickly slipped it back on the desk with a thud and got to his feet.

"Do you like the paperweight?" asked Mrs Stockwell. "It belonged to Richard's grandfather. A gift from his wife."

Tate shuffled in his seat awkwardly.

"Its workmanship is magnificent," he muttered, ashamed that he had considered pilfering it.

Georgina seemed unaware of his guilty secret and grinned and nodded at his approval of the thing.

"I believe we have come to a solution, Mr Tate. A suggestion, if you will. I shall let my advisor pitch the idea to you. Mr Cavendish?"

Gesturing for him to start his silver-tongued rescue of her business, her nausea worsened. Several gulps were needed to calm it.

Jon folded his arms and leaned against the edge of her desk alongside Mr Tate. She waited with bated breath. For a second, she was concerned that the supplier might be offended by his overly casual tone. The men in her circle of friends almost certainly would have raised their eyebrows at his body language. However, Cavendish's laid-back style appeared to relax Mr Tate, just as it did with her.

"Now, sir, what Mrs Stockwell stated about having to pay back her brother's debts is true. There is no question about it. You have my word that we had no idea what he was up to. She would have stopped him in his tracks if she had known about it sooner."

"I appreciate the kind words, and I thank you for them. But they are all only words. Words won't pay me back. I need my money."

Jon changed tack, inching a little closer, which inspired Mr Tate to do the same. Georgina was intrigued by Jon's manoeuvre, which seemed pre-planned to draw in the businessman and make him feel like he was in on a big secret.

"I understand. Can I be frank with you, Mr Tate?"

"Go on," said the businessman, as he leaned in closer still.

"Mr Duffield has damaged more than just our business connection with your organisation. He has driven away several vendors, just like your good self. Worse perhaps was the damage he did closer to home, taking out multiple loans in Mrs Stockwell's name. The cupboard is, let's say, 'bare'."

Georgina gasped. Why did Jon do that? How would this win him over, telling him she was broke and stupid? She tried to stomp her foot on his, hurl an object in his direction, prevent any more damage from coming from his mouth, but she couldn't. Instead, she had to sit there politely, watching it all unfold. At least Tate hadn't stormed out complaining about having his time wasted. Yet.

"I appreciate you might never want to deal with Stockwell's again, but I have a proposal for you. Until the debt is repaid, in full, with five per cent interest, Stockwell & Sons will pay a twenty per cent premium above the selling price."

"With interest?" Astonished, Georgina made an exclamation. "Mr Cav—"

Jon put his hand out like a policeman guiding traffic to silence her.

"With interest, sir. However, once the debt is repaid, Stockwell & Sons wants your product at twenty per cent below your selling price. Guaranteed for at least ten years."

Mr Tate furrowed his brows.

"Where did you pluck that twenty per cent discount from? That's hardly small change. With respect, why should I accept payments in instalments and lower my prices to a firm that has gladly defrauded me?"

"Because—"

By now, Jon was leaning in so close he was almost nose to nose with Tate.

"—Stockwell's will make you its sole hops supplier. Think for a minute. Currently, we are taking inferior hops from lots of suppliers in Herefordshire. But we will end our contracts with them and offer you our exclusive patronage. As you appreciate, a company of this size relying on a sole supplier puts their business at risk, but Mrs Stockwell and I know Stockwell & Sons can rely on the loyalty of Tate and Blackwell. Just like they have for decades before. It's time to return to the good old days, isn't it? Agreed?"

Mr Tate sat back in his chair, mulling over the offer.

Georgina sat there with her mouth gaping. The solution was so elegant. James had picked the inferior Herefordshire hops because it was cheaper. Now, Stockwell's would get better quality hops, but at the same price, thanks to the discount. Tate and Blackwell's would secure a sizeable regular order, and the beer would be the same superior quality once more. That would mean more orders from pubs and increased production. Every player in the ale market would end up in a virtuous circle. Stockwell's, Tate's, the pubs and the drinkers. His plan was pure genius.

Observing Mr Tate make the same mental calculations she had, she sat back and waited. She watched Jon patiently wait for his response. There was no doubt in his mind that he had sealed the deal. He had a look of pride about him without looking arrogant or shifty. As far as Georgina was concerned, Jon Cavendish would never be smug.

Upon seeing Mr Tate stand and shake Jon's hand so enthusiastically it looked like it might fall off, her heart nearly leapt out of her chest.

"We have a deal, sir."

After, he offered Georgina a more understated and chivalrous handshake.

"It is my pleasure to renew our business relationship with Stockwell & Sons. I will have my office prepare the paperwork and send it forthwith.

"Yes, please do, Mr Tate," she trilled.

He was escorted to his coach by Mr Bridges, who had no idea what had transpired except that the chap was in much better spirits than when he arrived. Georgina whipped her chair round to confront Jon.

"Jon, you played what I think you would call 'a blinder' there. You did it!"

She couldn't help but show her appreciation and relief by flinging her arms around his neck.

Jon laughed and returned her embrace.

"Steady on."

"Sorry," she blurted as she stepped back, red-faced.

"Don't worry yourself. I was more worried about poor Mr Bridges's delicate sensibilities."

"It's just... This is my first victory as I turn this ramshackle place around. And that's all down to you and your silver tongue."

"Well..." he joked, doing his best to look self-deprecating by tilting his head and sliding a finger around the inside of his shirt collar.

"I wish I knew how hops affect the quality of beer. I asked Mr McKay to get me some bottles to sample, but they are in a dark cupboard in the scullery still untouched."

He leaned his head to one side with that same contemplative look he had used when offering his proposal to Mr Tate.

"How about we go to the pub this evening?" he suggested. It probably wouldn't hurt to develop a taste for the stuff, even if you're a lady. I could help you."

"I've been in a pub before, I'll have you know," she protested with mock offence.

When he raised a brow in disbelief, she added sheepishly:

"Well, it was a Hertfordshire coaching inn, and I had wine, not ale."

"Thought so. Well, are you up for it then, a good old East End boozer?"

"Go on then," she said as they shook on the deal.

14

THE SAMPLING SESSION IN BETHNAL GREEN

It didn't make sense to him, but Jon was far more anxious about escorting Georgina to the boozer than he had been about meeting Mr Tate. On reflection, he thought it was for the best. If he was going to learn about ale production, it would stand her in good stead to learn about ale consumption.

Given the woeful state of the water from the standing taps, ale was a staple for the workers in London's East End, and Jon was no different. He liked his beer but wasn't a slave to it like other men. He'd seen too many men lose their homes, families and minds to it. He liked ales for their own sake, for the taste, rather than the effects. He loved to seek out bars frequented by the discerning drinker, packed with men with respectable professions and reputations amongst the working class. The brass hand pumps lined up at the bar were labelled with exotic names: 'India Pale Ale', 'Best Bitter' and 'Porter', rather than "ale," "gin," and "slops."

While Jon had always enjoyed his ale, his time at Stockwell & Sons had given him a newfound appreciation for the brewing process, and an understanding of his father's passion. For him, it was becoming more like alchemy, and it delighted him to be part of the industry. It was a rare and wonderful thing to understand the impact of roasting different grains on the final product, how hops influenced the flavour, and sugar the strength. Then there was the processing and the effect of temperature and humidity on the final product. It was the perfect blend of art and science.

He wanted Georgina to respect ale as much as he did. Stockwell & Sons was her brewery, but Jon decided it was up to him to show her how to truly love the product she helped make. He knew she could adapt her palate to appreciate the nuances of it. Could she learn to love it? And if not, could he make her love it?

His doubts were not from his ability to persuade. No, they came from his growing admiration for her. Georgina was special, one of a kind. Few women would be so willing to take over the burdens she did to restore the faith in her family business. Her sacrifices were immense, her struggles painful, yet she persevered. There was no woman he wanted more than her. She was delicate and elegant. Whenever she picked up a sack of grain, he thought her wiry limbs might snap under the strain. But, of course, they wouldn't. He knew as well as she did that underneath that brittle exterior was a constitution of iron, which was growing stronger by the day as each obstacle in her path was crushed, another problem solved. He did his best to ignore the growing attraction to her, telling himself he was there to work for her and nothing else—and it needed to stay that way.

At seven o'clock that evening, as the klaxon rang to signal the end of the shift, the day workers shuffled out, and the night shift's skeleton crew sauntered in. Jon awaited her by the bottom of the office stairs.

"You coming along then, son? Rachel's got a casserole on for us." David asked.

"I can't tonight, pa. I'm busy."

"Busy? You're not working late again, are you?"

Jon looked shifty.

"You're meeting a lass, aren't you? Haven't you broken enough hearts?" his father said as he fought to slide his arms into his heavily patched coat.

"I bet this week's pay packet that the girl in question is Mrs Stockwell, yes?"

Jon remained tight-lipped. It mattered not. His father didn't need to hear his response to know he was right.

"Oh, Jon, you big fool. You haven't got the best track record."

"What do you mean by that? Come on, let's hear it, pa."

"It's not a comment about you so much, son. It's just that you have that certain charm. The girls swoon after you like the rats behind the Pied Piper. Sometimes I think you forget. And then, when it's not reciprocated, they get hurt."

"Calm yourself, pa. I'm going out with Old Finnegan."

"So, you're not taking her out?" asked his father suspiciously.

"Alright, I am. But it's just business."

"Is that right?"

"Look, it's all above board. She's not a beer drinker, so she claims. But I reckon if she's going to make a real success of this place, she needs to know what makes a good ale. She needs to meet the people who drink her ale. Else, well, it's all a bit academic, I suppose. She's invested so much in my education. It's one of the few ways I can genuinely repay her for trusting me."

His father pondered and then nodded, even though he wasn't convinced.

"I take your point," he fibbed. "Well, make sure she tries a good stout. That Guinness is a fantastic seller. Fills the belly like a meal, and it takes the nip out of the air."

"Right you are, pa. See you soon."

Just after their conversation concluded, Georgina came downstairs. Unconsciously, Jon stood up straight, and his face took on his usual mischievous grin. As David Cavendish reached the heavy wooden doors, Jon looked around and saw his dad staring back at him. Even from that distance, the old man knew that look on his son's face. He narrowed his eyes as a warning his boy was under scrutiny from afar. Suddenly, Jon looked like a lad who had been wrongly accused of stealing sweets from the shop. David turned and left, his job done.

Jon had no intention of treating Georgina like his other East End girls. That promise would be easy to honour. He'd never met a woman as wonderful as Georgina Stockwell. His father was being a bit harsh on him. Most people would have considered his flirting harmless fun. Why not compliment a girl and make her blush and giggle? Make her feel good about herself? Surely, a bit of cheer was welcome on the mean streets of Whitechapel? He'd never falsely romanced a girl, taken advantage or broken her heart, unlike some of the other lads on Prospect Street.

Georgina was different. It wasn't just that she was a woman of high social standing or possessed dignity, grace and poise. He truly respected her as a person, not just as a boss. Treating her casually was unthinkable.

"Ready?" she enquired as she slid down the last step.

"When have you ever known me not to be ready for the pub?" he teased.

"This is not going to be a night of hard drinking like you used to go on with your docker friends," she said sternly.

He looked concerned.

"I'm pulling your leg," she chuckled. "Shall we? Oh, hang on a minute."

She reached in her back and fished out a tatty-looking grey cloak.

"I got Mr Bridges to pick it up for me. I thought I might blend in a bit more."

A smile spread across his face instinctively as he extended his elbow, preparing to escort her through the dark streets just as he would with his sisters. Instantly, he regretted it. Not because he was shunned, but because his gesture was warmly accepted. Didn't he just promise his father he wouldn't try to win Georgina over with his usual casual charm? When she put her slender ivory hand in the bend of his arm, he tried to pull away, but she wouldn't relinquish her grasp. Jon began to question if his father's concerns about his integrity were a premonition. He wondered where the night might go when they had both partaken in some ale sampling? As they left the brewery together, some of the chaps starting and ending their shifts spotted them and gave each other curious glances.

"So, Jon, where are you taking me?" she asked, her breath visible in the cold night air.

"I thought an inn might be the best place to start?" he said, then muttered, "I am not sure you're ready for The Little Drummer Boy just yet."

"The where?"

"Nothing.

"You'll love the Red Lion. It's a lovely traditional inn in Bethnal Green."

"Where's that?"

"Think of it as Whitechapel, but better. Well, relatively speaking."

She leaned in closer to him as they pushed through the jostling crowd, bumping into each other as they went about their business. He remembered her saying she seldom had walked anywhere in the past, and he was proud of how well she was adjusting.

"It's not far," he whispered as he put his other hand on top of hers and gave it a protective and reassuring squeeze. "The Red Lion may not be as fine as the establishments you're used to frequenting, but they offer a fine assortment of beers and spirits. Better than what's normally served around here, that's for sure."

"And what is normally served?"

"Our lot tend to go for anything cheap and strong. Gin mainly. You can't blame folks for the hard drinking, I suppose. Life isn't easy here. Wanting to escape the hardship with a drink is a popular pastime."

"A bit like those poor souls of Hogarth's in his sketch of Gin Lane?"

"Exactly," Jon second-guessed, despite never having seen any of the famous painter's work, wishing he hadn't lumped himself in with 'our lot'.

When they were together, the class divide melted away, and he preferred not to remind her. He'd met one or two 'posh birds' in his time, mainly those on the voyeuristic guided tours of the tenements, but she was nothing like them, with their fake philanthropy and pretty frills. They looked down on the impoverished residents of the East End with contempt and strutted around haughtily. Never, ever would they fight the underclass's corner as emphatically as Georgina. She treated him as an equal, a person. Jon allowed himself to wonder if it was affection or her philosophy on life that made him feel so special.

As they reached the main road in front of the brewery, Georgina's coachman was ready to take her home.

"Ah, Mr Glazer. There's been a change of plan. Did Mr McKay not give you my message?"

"No, ma'am, I've not been back since lunchtime. Mrs Duffield had me on errands all afternoon."

Georgina flinched at the mention of her mother. Mr Glazer gave a concerned stare towards the pair of them.

These days the kids in the area were used to seeing the fancy carriage, and they no longer stood in awe. However, a few ragged little ones continued to reach out, begging for a bit of loose change. Without attracting too much attention, the driver handed the tallest lad a thruppenny bit, and then the youngsters scampered away with their haul as the other onlooker kids gasped and whispered.

Georgina tried hard not to look like she'd been delighted to see her coachman's benevolence, but Jon knew that she was.

"Just a moment," she told her companion as she peeled her hand from his elbow.

Approaching the carriage, the coachman leaned over. She spoke quietly as Jon hung back. The man's eyes looked at him and narrowed, just like his father's had earlier. He looked at the curious threadbare cloak around his mistresses' shoulders and wondered what was going on.

"Mr Cavendish," she called out, "I am right in thinking I can hire a cab to take me home this evening, can I not?"

"Yes, Mrs Stockwell. Quite easily. There will be plenty of them around."

Jon could see that this was no reassurance to the coachman. Both men knew there were a dozen charlatans for every fine, upstanding cabbie, especially in that part of London.

"Sir, I shall personally see to it that Mrs Stockwell is brought home safely," he told Glazer. "Even if I have to walk her to her doorstep myself."

His promise seemed only to deepen the coachman's mistrust, but since Georgina was insistent for Glazer to 'stop fussing', the man had little choice but to comply. Tipping his matt black top hat to his mistress, he snapped the reins, and the two black horses and the matching black carriage clattered away along the cobbles.

"He ain't keen on leaving you with me, is he?"

"No, he's not. Glazer has always looked out for me. More so since Richard passed away."

Jon looked down at his secondhand outfit, not shabby but nowhere near as nice as the neatly pressed coachman's uniform.

"Why should he trust me?" said Jon, uncharacteristically downbeat, as he watched a particularly grubby-looking chap slouch past. "He doesn't know me from that fella there, does he?"

"No. Perhaps not. But it doesn't matter. You have my trust. Now, will we finally sample this fantastic ale you've promised me?"

He extended his arm once more, and they strolled northwards along Commercial Road.

Bethnal Green was one of London's primary textile regions. The mill workers were savouring an hour's respite before returning to their cold, dark family homes or lodging houses, so the boozer was lively on their arrival. The clientele were coarse, unwashed, and uncouth, but they were far more civilised than anything likely to be encountered in the pubs and gin palaces near Jon's tenement. When they had left, the middle-class men would take their place, coming in for a drink and a chat after their evening meals.

"Ah, Jon Cavendish, as I live and breathe," yelled the landlord, a lively, larger-than-life character who was both tall and fat. "How you diddlin', me old mucker?"

"Grand, Pete, grand," said Jon with a nod. "Even better now, I am in your fine establishment."

"It's been a while since we last saw you. The missus thought you'd vanished. She said you'd probably stowed away on a ship to some exotic port."

"Nah. I got myself a new job. A permanent one. On my best behaviour and all that. Staying late to impress the boss, wasn't I," he chuckled.

The bartender laughed heartily at the joke. Georgina dug him in the ribs under her cloak.

"I'll just get us a seat over there, then I'll be back."

"Right, you are, Jon. Good to see ya, fella. It really is."

Jon ushered Georgina over to a quieter area around the corner, with a table near a tiny window. He sat facing the wall, and she sat opposite, with a good view of their location.

He stared at Georgina as she sat down. She gazed around the room with wide eyes, partly like a frightened bird, partly like a kid in a sweet shop. The light accentuated the rosy flush on her cheeks from the brisk walk out in the cold. His charming grin lit up his face as much as the gas lamps.

"What does that smile mean?"

"Nothing."

"So, finally, am I going to get this ale you've been promising?"

"Soon. Be patient for once. I realise the purpose of our visit is to try the beer, but I think we ought to have a meal first. That is rule number one when it comes to drinking. Be sure to eat before heading out for a night, or else it will go straight to your head. The mutton stew is delicious here."

"Are you fattening me up for Christmas, Jon?" she joked. "Plum pudding this morning and now a casserole. Actually, it reminds me of one thing mother and I agreed on."

"Which is?"

Georgina stuck her nose up in the air and put on her best haughty voice.

"A corset might fix a woman's waistline, but it won't fix a double chin."

"I bet she doesn't say that," he chuckled as he turned and bellowed towards the bar. "Pete! Two casseroles over here when you're ready, mate. And two halves of Fullers! Thanks, squire!"

His attention turned back to Georgina.

"Yes, she does. Amongst other things like when I would find another husband."

"What does your pa say to that? All the expense of a second society wedding must have him grumbling?"

"He seldom speaks. He feels my mother says enough for both of them, to be honest. He learned many years ago that if he wants a quiet life, it's best to agree with everything she says from the get-go."

"That's a shame. My father dotes on my younger siblings. And the grown-up me, when I let him get away with it."

"We'll always be children in our parent's eyes, I suppose. Your home sounds very loving."

"It is," he smiled, "I think Archie was my ma's favourite, secretly, of course. And 1 was her cherished first-born son. We were happy."

He looked a little sad. He hadn't really told her much about his ma.

"We *are* happy," he corrected.

"You must miss her," she hinted, but she could see he wanted to change the subject. "It sounds like you have it all, Jon Cavendish. A close family who thinks the world of each other."

"You have a family too, just a different type of family. You have taken running the brewery in your stride. Despite the odds, your employees hold you in even greater esteem every day. And they are men! They must secretly idolise you, you know."

The talk was getting serious, so it was Jon's turn to lighten the mood.

"Plus, you live in that poncy house in that fancy neighbourhood, Mayfair. And love a duck. If you ever tire of it, there's always that rural estate up north."

"What makes you think I own a rural residence—up north or anywhere?"

"Toffs always have rural estates. Either cold grey castles that have been in the family for years or those mock-Tudor merchant houses that fool no one."

"It seems you have a good grasp of second homes, Jon. Actually, I don't own a manor house nestled in a rolling landscape meticulously planned by Capability Brown."

Her voice tailed off as she muttered to herself, "well, not any longer." She thought he hadn't heard her over all the noise, but he had. There was no way he would let the comment slide.

"I sold it," she said, giving him a flat look.

"Sold it?"

"Yes."

It dawned on him why the property was no longer hers.

"..to give you the money to keep the factory afloat?"

She nodded.

"You poor thing, Georgina. I'm so sorry. As if your life hasn't been challenging enough already. Chin up. You must be due a lucky break soon."

"There's nothing to apologise for, and I don't believe in luck—good or bad," but the remorse in her eyes belied her words.

She paused, staring at the gentle glow from the gaslight on the wall and was relieved when Pete's barmaid swooped over with the food. Soon, a tray with two large bowls and two small glasses of ale filled their fields of view, puncturing the moment's intensity, but Georgina was soon trapped again like a rabbit in a snare. Jon's earnest face would quickly compel her to divulge more.

"Here you go! Enjoy."

"The meal looks nice," said Georgina, feeling able to comment on the food but very unsure about the ale.

"We've never had a bad meal here. The wife of the bartender is an excellent cook. Before marrying him, she was a maid for a wealthy household who lived near the entrance to Hyde Park, not far from Wellington's house."

"Is that right?"

"Aye."

Georgina appeared to be suitably impressed.

"So, tell me more about this country pile? Please? I do realise it can't be easy," he said softly.

"Yes, it was a beautiful home, and I liked visiting there to have a break from the bustling city, but I manage perfectly well without it. I am sure I can stay at a hotel or visit a friend if I want to see more of England's green and pleasant land. You see, it was more Richard's family's than mine. And since I am the only one left, all the blood relatives have passed on now—well, there was no one to sell it back to."

She paused, her gaze fixed on her spoon, stirring her stew.

"To be honest, he would have preferred that I sell it. He was never sentimental about things like that. Apart from me, only the brewery meant something to him. It needed the investment more than I needed another house to rattle around in alone. I can only live in one at any one time, after all."

"What a selfless act," he remarked.

"Oh, not that selfless. I thought I could treat myself to lots of new floaty frilly outfits with whatever was left over."

He giggled at her optimistic nature.

"Still, how noble it was of you to sell it off so that folks like my pa can stay employed."

She relaxed in her chair and stared at him for a while.

"Well, it so happens that I agree with you— although I wouldn't quite call it noble. I was forced to do it because of James's antics, or I never would have parted with it, I suppose. Anyway, enough of that. Let's stop moping about. I've eaten that stew and sipped at this beer. How about you tell me more about it, then buy us another round?"

"Are you sure you can handle it? I think I'd better make them half pints again!" he said with a cheeky wink.

Jon slipped away to place their next drink orders with Pete at the bar.

"Here," Jon said, pushing the first glass of the amber liquid forward.

"That looks familiar, I think," she said, examining the hue.

"Take a sip. This is called 'small beer'."

She bent down and peered at the side of the glass, then lifted it carefully and sipped from it. Her curious expression gave Jon a chuckle. She obviously didn't like it and was trying hard not to express her displeasure.

"It's not to your taste," he laughed.

"The floaty bits are a bit off-putting."

"Extra flavour", he said.

She took another sip.

"Keep it on your tongue and see if you can taste that touch of bitterness in there. Like that stuff Finnegan had you sniffing."

"Do you know, I can," she chirped after swirling the drink in her mouth and gulping it down.

"Hops play a significant role in the production of beer. The higher the quality of the hops, the more prominent the bitterness."

"But why's it called small beer? Seems an odd name to me."

"It doesn't last long, so it's best consumed quickly, that's all. Nothing to do with the size of the measures it's served in. This is the sort of stuff people would make at home since the Middle Ages."

She smiled as she surveyed the room, trying to understand how popular the brew might be.

"Do we brew small beer?"

"My pa stated we did, but Mr Duffield stopped making it when sales started to slide."

"Probably because he started using second-rate hops?"

She sent him a knowing glance, hoping she was right. He gave a non-committal shrug.

"I'm ashamed to admit that I don't know as much as you do about this," she said, looking down at the beer and swirling it around in the glass.

"I've spent a lot more time on the factory floor chatting to the staff. You've been staring at sales figures and quotes for the repairs."

"Thank you for being my eyes and ears and finding a use for that connoisseur's palate you've developed when it comes to ale."

He cracked a grin, and their gaze remained locked for a few seconds.

"Pete said they used to buy Stockwell's, but now they've switched to Simmonds and Hunter because of quality concerns," he says.

Georgina looked glum.

"Cheer up. You were right. It was the damp hops that caused the problem. It ruined the stock, but James used it in many more batches. Of course, the punters got wise to it and bought something else. The pubs ended up throwing gallons away and stopped buying anymore."

Georgina paused for thought as she sipped from her glass again. She wrinkled her nose and set it down.

"Let me help you with that," he said before snatching the glass and chugging down the remainder.

He gave Pete a signal, and the two empty glasses were swiftly replaced with two more, this time filled with a darker liquid.

"Now, this here is what is known as a bitter. It's a type of pale ale. One of the darker ones."

She cautiously examined the glass held aloft between them.

"I think it's a lovely shade," she remarked, "as for the taste—"

He laughed as she grimaced.

"I'll have no dissent in the ranks, miss. You told me you wanted to learn about ale and learn you shall. Have a little taste."

She sipped at it cautiously.

"Well, I suppose it's better than the other one," she protested.

"Most bitters don't have so much hops," he explained. "And they have a wide range of strengths, with the light ales being the weakest and the best bitters the strongest."

Georgina managed about half of the bitter before Jon swept in again to finish it off.

The next shade was a deep reddish brown.

"And this one?"

"Brown ale," he said.

She took another sniff and a sip.

"This is sweeter? Correct?"

"That one has less alcohol in it. It's not very popular these days. The brown malt is expensive to source. Pale malt is a lot cheaper to produce, and the yield is higher too."

The final one was so dark that it was practically black. Georgina examined it as though it were impossible that it was drinkable.

"Is this liquid tar?" she joked.

"Stout. It's our most popular beer. Well, it is now it's being made with better quality ingredients."

Georgina crinkled her eyes as she pressed the rough glass to her soft mouth. She sipped at it slowly, then licked away the foam moustache she felt on her upper lip.

"I find it appealing," she said.

Jon's mouth sprang open in amazement.

"What is that? Is that a bitter, nutty taste I detect? A bit like the syrup in a crème caramel?"

"Possibly, if I knew what one of those was. That taste is the malt, or maybe it's oats? Even I get confused. You're right. There is so much to learn!" he chortled.

He took a sip, raised the glass and admired the brew.

"This is made here in the inn. Pete has a special licence to make it."

"Pubs can make their own ale? Well, I never. Seems I have more competition than I thought."

She took a second, more substantial gulp, leaving a deep mottled white stripe around the sides of the glass, then knocked back the rest.

"Steady on, girl," he said before a huge belly laugh.

"Actually, Mr Cavendish, this one is rather moreish. I'm wondering whether you'd like me to get us two whole pints?"

"Well, only if you think it's a good idea. I suppose it is research after all!" he said heartily.

Jon noticed that Georgina's strong preference for the stout showed no signs of abating. As the night progressed, one drink led to another, and soon the table was a mass of empty glasses.

"Oh, go on, you spoil sport. Just one more, Jon!"

"No!"

"Well, a half then?"

"No. You'll have a sore head in the morning, as it is," he lamented.

"I don't care."

"Well, I do. Mr McKay will string me up if he sees you in this state!"

"What, state?" she slurred gently.

"Come on, Georgina. Time to head home. I'll get a bottle of stout for you to have when you get home? How about that?"

"What-o! But of course!" she shrieked.

Georgina was looking worse for wear by the time they left, and Jon was starting to regret buying as many drinks as he had. He'd overlooked her slight frame and infrequent drinking. He was reasonably sure he'd never seen a girl that wobbly in years. Not since Milly Compton and Henry Kirkham got married.

Once they were on the pavement, Jon's head spun round, looking for a taxi. Georgina retook his arm, but this time rather than just politely placing her hand on it, she used it more like the staircase bannister.

"I think we should travel together in a taxi,
Georgina. We can't fit both of us in a sedan chair."

"Fiddlesticks, I'd rather walk," she announced as
the knees of her jelly-legs knocked together.
"Mayfair is only a few miles away."

"Only a few miles. Gee whiz, that's great," said Jon
under his breath.

She gave him a flirtatious look.

"I consider myself to be a highly skilled walker.
How about you?"

Their sweet expressions were mutual as she spun on her heels to move her face in front of his. Their mouths were inches apart, and their eyes locked on each other. Jon restrained himself just in time from giving her a delicate kiss. She was his boss, and she'd been drinking. His father's warning stuck in his mind.

"I like to stroll, myself," he said as he manoeuvred
her out of the danger zone. "Ready?"

"Ready."

They walked for quite some time in silence, happy to be in each other's company. Jon was pleased the fresh air and exercise was sobering Georgina up a little. Once she felt steadier on her feet, he decided it best to turn the conversation back to business.

"You know, I've been thinking. You've been investing a lot of time and money trying to salvage the business, putting right the wrongs of James, and I admire you for that, I really do. But if pubs can brew their own ale under licence, and their pubs are packed with punters happy to drink good quality Mann's, Youngs, and Fuller's beer that they can buy in, it's going to be an uphill struggle to get them to change back to Stockwell's. It would be like asking them to take a step backwards?"

"Indeed. What we need is a fresh approach," she said confidently.

"Yes."

Then there was a long silence.

"Do you have a plan, Jon? Please, you're my advisor. Tell me what to do to win them over."

The silence continued until she started to giggle.

"What's so amusing?" he asked.

"I should drink stout more often. It gives me special powers. Although my mother might disagree, of course."

Jon looked confused.

"Shall I put you out of your misery, young man?"

"Please—"

"Well, if we can't get our beer back into the pubs using our traditional ales, we shall infiltrate them with a new one. A brand new exciting flavour they've never tried before. We give them an experience like I've had tonight—"

"Drinking too much stout in a strange place with a strange man?"

"No, silly. We offer them the best-tasting Christmas ale they have ever tasted. No other brewery has come up with a viable product that I have seen advertised, and the men in pubs like that won't be happy with a yuletide staple like eggnog or a mulled wine."

"Go on."

"The idea came to me when I could taste the bitter crème caramel flavour in the stout. How about a stout with a chocolate or mincemeat note— something Christmassy!"

"It could work. Stout is your best seller at the moment—"

"—And all we have to do is enhance the flavour just a little to get people talking about it—" she said with a knowing look.

"—and then the punters will be asking all the landlords to stock it."

"By Jove, I think he's got it!" Georgina teased.

"We could do a full-page ad in the Pall Mall Gazette! Perhaps mention that a woman was in charge of developing the product?"

"I'd rather you didn't."

"Why not?"

"You've never run out of toilet paper in your house, have you?" he teased. "People cut it into squares for the outside privy!"

"They do?" she asked with a concerned expression. "Alright, let's have posters at the mainline stations? Better?"

"Much better," he said. "And we can have street sellers giving away free tasters near the station entrances. If any of the costers complain about losing a pitch, we can give them a few bottles to keep them sweet. Actually, tasting the product will be much better than wasting money on newspaper adverts. With a bit of luck, we can ask a journalist to do a feature on how we make it. Then you'll get coverage for free."

Georgina threw her free hand in the air with glee. Finally, she was beginning to see a way out of the mess.

"This is a magnificent idea, Jon. I just know it. You must assemble the workers and the master brewers to do a taste test. We can make some small batches just like Pete does, get some feedback and make it the best ale in the whole of London."

As she smiled up at him, his face tipped down. Jon was sure he was staring at the face of an angel, albeit still slightly inebriated. He stifled the urge to kiss her again.

The more the ale wore off, the faster Georgina began to walk. She had not exaggerated when she told him she was a keen walker. The brisk pace was starting to make Jon's legs burn, and engaging with Georgina's relentless chatter made his lungs strain. Still, he was disappointed to turn into her Mayfair street.

She looked at him when they were finally standing on her front step. A beautiful glow adorned her face, gently lit by the gaslight above. She looked lovely, wholesome, and everything a gorgeous woman should be. As she gazed up at him, her eyes glittered with excitement. Jon avoided reaching for her waist by stuffing his hands deep into his pockets.

Off in his peripheral vision, he caught sight of the parlour curtain rustling. Mr McKay was monitoring his every move.

"Thank you for a wonderful and productive evening. I can't wait for us to start working on our flagship Christmas ale. Shall I send for my coach to take you to your home?"

"Don't trouble Mr Glazer at this time of night for me. I'll enjoy a bit more of a stroll on this lovely night."

His words clung to the cold air in a thick mist.

"Are you sure?"

"Absolutely."

He took a step back and down onto the pavement. Their heads were in perfect alignment.

She leaned in towards him. Jon tilted his head to one side, anticipating a peck on the cheek. He was wrong. She caught him on the corner of his mouth, and he was sure she had done it on purpose.

He tilted his head once again in her direction and held his breath as she brushed her lips against his, with more purpose this time. It was the softest and nicest kiss he'd ever experienced. He put his hands in his pockets and locked his elbows.

She broke off the caress and took a step back while he was still reeling from the delight of it. Her expression reflected the shock she felt at the boldness of her actions.

As she uttered a startled 'G'night', quickly unlocked the door and disappeared inside without a backward glance, laughing nervously all the time.

Several seconds passed in silence as Jon peered at the locked door in front of him, gently touching his face, before he turned and walked each and every mile back to his home in Whitechapel with the broadest of grins.

15

'ARE YOU ALRIGHT MA'AM?'

The gravity of what she'd just done hit Georgina the moment she shut her front door. She leaned against it, hands pressed hard towards the wood as if barricading herself in. Her breath was shallow, partly due to excitement, partly due to panic. She'd kissed Jon Cavendish! Fully. What had gotten into her?

"Ma'am?"

At that late hour, Mr McKay's sudden presence startled her.

"Are you all right, madam?"

"Fine. Although you sneaking up on me like that wasn't one of your better ideas."

"I'm sorry. It's just with you stuck to the door like that, I thought I'd better check."

"Thank you for your concern, Mr McKay."

"I hope you had a good evening? Mr Glazer advised you were being escorted by Mr Cavendish and might return late. I felt it wise to wait up to make sure you got back safely."

"Well, here I am, safe and sound. And yes, it was a delightful evening. I believe we have found the last piece of the puzzle in turning round the brewery's fortunes."

"I see, ma'am. Would you like a nightcap?"

He looked at her strangely, and she worried for a second that he'd guessed what had happened between them, or worse, seen.

"May I take your cloak? I don't recall seeing it before? Is it new?"

"New to me. Mr Bridges got it for me, so I might blend into Whitechapel when I am on an errand in the area."

"Are you sure that's wise, Miss Georgina? Shouldn't you be sending the men out on errands for you?"

"Not if that errand involves me drinking in a Bethnal Green pub to sample the ales of my competitors."

McKay's chin almost hit the floor.

"I appreciate you buying those bottles for me to try, but I realised they would never taste the same as quaffing them in the ambience of what Mr Cavendish calls 'a proper East End boozer'. He was right. I'm heading to bed. Could you please inform Sarah that her presence is not needed? It's far too late for her to be up and about. I shall cope perfectly well on my own."

"As you wish, ma'am. May I bring something up for you? Maybe some brandy or a hot chocolate?"

By then, she was already on her way upstairs.

"Perhaps a brandy. Would you mind warming the glass? It is rather chilly tonight."

"Yes, ma'am. I shall knock on the door and leave your drink on a tray for you."

The phrase "Wonderful, Mr McKay. Thank you so much," wafted down the stairs just before her door softly closed.

Once back in her room, she wondered if David Cavendish would give Jon a grilling when he finally got back.

She sank down on the corner of her bed and fought to undo her boot laces. It gave her plenty of time to reflect on her surprising actions that night. The ale undoubtedly played a significant role in the way things unfolded. But then again, the mutual attraction was becoming harder to deny. The stout merely pointed out the elephant in the room sooner rather than later.

The walk's brisk air hadn't done much to quell the feeling of freedom and joyous recklessness that pulsed through her veins. If she were honest, she had played up how tipsy she looked. She had felt reasonably normal by the time they reached Whitechapel underground station. But her little white lie with her behaviour was just enough to allow her to skirt the boundaries of her professional relationship with him.

She tried to remember how long she had wanted to kiss him. Was it when he brokered the deal with Mr Tate? Or perhaps when she had seen him shirtless, grafting away to move stock in the warehouse. Who knew?

She was glad the stout had given her the courage to undertake her covert operation and find out how he felt about her. The results had been rather spectacular.

True to his word, Mr McKay knocked politely on the door and left a large measure of brandy for her to enjoy.

She lay back on her bed and sipped the tingly warm liquid. She cringed at the thought of the first fumbling peck on his lips but decided that the proper kiss had been fantastic. She also told herself he wanted to do it just as much as she did, else why tilt his head to make it easier for her. And, oh, those butterflies. Those wonderful, tingly butterflies she'd not felt in years. There was another sip of brandy, a larger one this time. She was still dizzy thinking about how his lips had parted slightly to make room for hers. It wasn't a passionate or intense kiss, unlike how she used to kiss Richard when they were first married, but it still had the power to make her heart pound and her body tingle right down to her feet.

As she finished the last of the lovely warm brandy and snuggled into her cosy bed, she hoped neither of them would feel regret in the morning and prayed their next encounter would be as relaxed and natural as it had always been.

15

THE SLOW RIDE TO WHITECHAPEL

When Georgina woke, she instantly felt sickened, not by a hangover, but by deep regret.

There was none of the polite chit-chat with Mr Glazer as the coach made its way to the brewery. Georgina stared out of the window, looking more like a lifeless shop dummy being transported to Whiteley's department store, than a person.

Much like her first day, she stepped out of the coach with trepidation and strode across the goods inward yard and off towards her office. She took a deep breath as she pushed the heavy wooden door open, expecting all eyes to be on her once again, but the men carried on with their work, not batting an eyelid about her arrival.

She put her head down and walked briskly again, pretending to adjust the pleats of her skirt. Just as she got to the foot of the stairs, she recognised the shoes on the bottom step, Jon Cavendish's shoes.

She shook the tresses of hair from her face and looked up. His grin was as broad as a Cheshire cat's. Georgina felt even sicker. What if he was grinning because he had bragged about the kiss? Or made it sound like more!

She cast quick looks across the room once again, but her arrival still hadn't registered on their faces. He leaned in towards her ear.

"How's your head this morning?"

"I'll have you know that my head is functioning perfectly well," she replied with a snappy, excessively formal tone.

"Right. Glad to hear it," Jon said with a small frown on his face, as she barged past him.

A few steps later, she turned back to face him.

"Mr Cavendish, would you gather all the master brewers and have them join us in my office?"

"Us? Me as well?"

"Of course, you as well. Who else would be better at evangelising about the Stockwell Christmas Ale strategy?"

As she continued up the steps, she became aware of Jon's eyes on her. It felt good, but not enough to ease her worries about the sudden turn their relationship had taken. She maintained her composure and regained her pride with each pace until she reached her door. Then she slipped back into thinking about how they might move on from the kiss if they decided there was no future for them.

All of the master brewers filed in at nine fifteen on the dot. Jon closed the door behind them. The men looked at her with respect. In the short time she had been there, she had always kept her word and never let them down. Their working relationship was now one of trust and respect and nothing like the rancorous one under James.

They had known for a while that she was approachable whenever there was a problem, an idea, or a recommendation, no matter how unpalatable or unexpected it might seem. Her benevolent management style was welcome. She was getting better at prioritising and improving the brewery's efficiency as it limped back to full production. Rather than dreading being summoned, they were eager for her to share what was on her mind.

"Gentlemen, how nice to see you all. Thank you for taking the time to attend. I shall keep this brief, I promise."

She circled from behind her desk and took a position in front of them.

"So, what, is it, Mrs Stockwell," David Cavendish piped up. "We are itching to know, ain't we lads."

She looked at the row of men fidgeting like school boys in front of the headmaster.

"There's nothing to worry about. It is good news. Mr Cavendish and I, Jon Cavendish that is, have been considering how we might revitalise the company now the cards are more stacked in our favour."

There was an expectant murmur amongst the master brewers.

"Reviving public interest in Stockwell & Sons will require much more than just a return to producing our excellent ales. When people lost faith in our beers, they found new ones, ales that are now their favourites, ales they won't want to swap from, especially after such a poor experience with us."

The men were nodding and whispering amongst themselves.

"Very true, Mrs Stockwell," said Old Finnegan.

"Aye," David continued. "There was more to Stockwell & Sons than just decent beer. We were well-liked and respected for producing honest ales at an honest price. When Mr Duffield started with his corner cutting and economising and rubbing all the suppliers up the wrong way, well, that was the beginning of the end."

"Quite. The door on how we used to do business, rightly or wrongly, is now firmly closed. A new approach is needed, and that is what I want to speak to you about today, an approach I believe will work well."

"Go on," said Finnegan.

"Since we cannot get the drinkers to switch to a similar ale, we will offer them something new. Something delicious and exquisite. A treat, the likes of which they have never had before."

"Like what?" asked David. "Can't we just offer a discount on the stout?"

"I am afraid not, Mr Cavendish. No, now is the time to be bold and radical. We will reignite their interest in our beer and showcase the quality of our craftsmanship with a special ale—a Christmas ale.

What better time to relaunch ourselves? The festive season is almost upon us, and I know Stockwell & Sons can make a premium yuletide beer. Other companies have dabbled with the idea, but no one has made something exceptional. I want you to work together to make us a new recipe that is truly special. What do you say?"

The cheering was deafening. David Cavendish dashed over to his son and ruffled his hair playfully.

"That's a Bobby Dazzler of an idea, Jon!"

"Gentlemen," he said, raising his voice, "the idea was Mrs Stockwell's and hers alone. I merely gave her a little guidance on some minor points."

Georgina felt her face burn with a mix of joy, pride, affection and embarrassment.

"What I need from you, my wonderful master brewers, is to produce a winning formula. I think we are all agreed a limited edition stout offers the path of least resistance to this new brew, yes?"

"Aye, Mrs Stockwell," they yelled.

"We need something dark, with a good quality malt," said David.

"Chocolate malt," said one of the most experienced brewers, Walter Sanders.

Eric Watts poked Walter in the shoulder and mocked him.

"You and your chocolate malt. You're obsessed with it!"

"Rightly so. When I make my batches at home, my family loves it."

"Tell me more, Walter. Does it have chocolate in it?"

"Nah, Mrs Stockwell," he said with a smile. "It means we roast the malt til it goes really dark. It has chocolatey notes, but there ain't no chocolate in it."

"Oh, I see," she said, trying not to look baffled.

"Yeah, but Mann's do a chocolate stout sometimes. Would chocolate on its own make it different enough for our purposes?"

 "What about a bit of juniper? Or cloves? Or cinnamon? The sort of stuff you get in a mulled wine, but not as strong?"

"Spices are expensive," warned Jon, "When the spice clippers come into dock, there's hell to pay if any of their cargo falls overboard. Whatever we pick needs to be festive and reasonably cheap to produce."

"If that's the case, it must be the cloves," said Eric Watts.

As their excitement became more palpable, Georgina's optimism soared.

"Gentlemen, I can see you all have some wonderful suggestions. Now, we must make sense of them. Remember, we need something with maximum taste, maximum profits, minimal production difficulty, and something to pique the interest of drinkers. Please split off into small groups for a few minutes and put together some suggestions with rough costs. Jon, please hand out these notepads and pencils."

A little while later, the suggested recipes were handed in, and each one was voted on as a group.

The consensus was a stout brewed with a high proportion of chocolate malt, with no hops, and flavoured with a few cloves, a hint of juniper berries, and a touch of pepper.

"Now, I'd like each team to make one barrel, adapting the recipe as you see fit. Then we shall have a tasting competition, and the best tasting ale will go into full production. I appreciate this experiment must be done out of hours. I will pay you for your time and make sure there is an evening meal for each of you—and we shall hold a party in the courtyard to celebrate the relaunch, and your close family will be invited. Agreed?"

"Aye, Mrs Stockwell!" They cheered again.

"Jon, now we have the basic concept, can you think about how you will spread the word? We need to knock the landlords and the punters bandy with this ale. We can't afford to miss a trick. We're relying on you."

"Yes, Mrs Stockwell. It will be my pleasure."

Excited about the prospect of the new lifeline for Stockwell's, the master brewers traipsed down the stairs to get to work on the recipe.

"Jon," Georgina called as he trailed them out. "I wonder if you might stay behind for a moment? I'd like to discuss our next steps."

Jon hung back as requested. The look his father gave him was easy to decipher. Either he had told his father what happened the night before, or David Cavendish had guessed something might be developing between them.

"Mr Bridges, would you mind popping down to the canteen and getting Mr Cavendish and me a coffee? I am parched, and my throat feels terribly dry. Get one for yourself too."

"Of course, Mrs Stockwell. Thank you."

Once Mr Bridges was gone, she took a deep breath, then walked towards Jon.

"Erm—about last night."

"What about it?"

His innocent expression made it difficult for Georgina to maintain her professional distance.

"Come now. You know what I mean. I feel I owe you an apology. You have my word. It won't happen again. Now, can we please forget about it and get back to concentrating on the Christmas ale launch?"

"No problem. Mum's the word," he said with a wink.

"I mean it, Jon. Please do not make me feel worse about it than I already do. We're colleagues and nothing more. I would like things to stay that way."

"Yes, Mrs Stockwell. I shall respect your request. It's all forgotten."

"Good."

Mr Bridges returned, struggling to negotiate the closed door with an armful of coffees.

Georgina opened it, took two steaming mugs from Mr Bridges, and then handed one to Jon.

She was not sure if Jon was play-acting or genuine when he agreed to them going back to being colleagues again. His fingers brushed against hers when she handed him the drink, and he gave her a cheeky wink when Mr Bridges wasn't looking. Her stomach somersaulted all over again.

17

AGAINST BETTER JUDGEMENT

There was no way Jonathan Cavendish was going to forget that night. As for Georgina, he wasn't going to let her forget it either. It wasn't that big a deal. He let himself get too close to her despite his better judgement telling him not to. But he'd made that decision before he knew she was interested in him. Things were different now.

Every time she handed him a paper to review, he'd let his fingertips brush against hers, relishing the way her cheeks flushed despite her best efforts to keep them cool. When he saw she was heading in his direction, he playfully blocked her path, making it impossible for her to avoid colliding with him. Throughout the day, they would steal looks at one another and secretly grin. With time, these clandestine encounters became more frequent.

There was no surprise to Jon that their first proper kiss outside her Mayfair home was to be the first of many.

It began when Mr Bainbridge, Georgina's financial advisor, came to Stockwell & Son's one chilly, blustery day in late November. It had just gone noon when the mild-mannered businessman trotted towards the office, briefcase in hand, greeting everyone he saw with a kind word.

He was only there for a short while, perhaps ten minutes, but it was long enough to change everything.

Out on the factory floor, Jon watched Bainbridge's entrance as he cleaned out the still. The first batch of India pale ale made with Kentish hops from Tate and Blackwell was ready. To get his attention, his father had to cuff his ear so that Jon would concentrate on the task at hand. In Jon's opinion, Georgina and Bainbridge had endured an unpleasant encounter. The elderly man paced across the factory floor, shaking his head on his way out. Soon after, Georgina left her office, flew down the stairs, and retreated to the fermenting cellar.

After waiting for a good ten minutes without seeing her return, Jon took a lamp and descended to the cellar to see if she was alright.

"Georgina?" he yelled down to the basement.

"I'm here," came a voice from the shadows.

He walked slowly down the ramshackle wooden steps and traced his way along the long, dingy wall. At the opposite end, he could just make her out, perched on some upturned tea chests.

"Georgina? What's up? Why are you here on your own?"

"I'm thinking."

"About what? Did Mr Bainbridge upset you? Shove up a bit, eh?"

He placed the lamp on the new flagstones and took a seat next to her on a crate.

"He didn't upset me."

"So, what then? Tell me."

She let out a heavy sigh. He correctly deduced he would need to give her some time to divulge her secret.

"Mother has upset me. She insists that I find a new manager for the brewery and step down from my current role. Mr Bainbridge has been tasked with identifying suitably qualified applicants. He gave me a shortlist just now, then left."

Jon felt a knot form in his belly.

"I take it you're not going to go along with this ludicrous scheme?"

"No. I was a bit harsh when I boxed Mr Bainbridge's ears. Of course, he was just the messenger, but he took the brunt of my rage. I made it quite clear to him that my mother's proposal was unacceptable. Now, he has the unenviable task of explaining to mother dearest that her plan has failed. As you can imagine, he was not happy about that. But since I pay his fees and she doesn't, he had to side with me."

"Poor chap."

"Yes, I do feel sorry for him. She can be so brutal when she doesn't get her own way."

"But that's his problem now. You are still in charge of this place, yes? So why the long face?"

"Well, I might have succeeded in halting the recruiting of a man to replace me, but I have only won the battle, not the war. Mr Bainbridge will inform my mother of my decision, and I will be summoned to speak with her shortly."

"So? You can handle that, surely!"

"Once she gets a bee in her bonnet about something, she won't let it go. She will move back to Mayfair and work day and night to grind me down into submission. I'll be removed from the company and married off again in two shakes of a lamb's tail. I've never been able to assert my will when it conflicts with hers. And after all the stress and strain of turning this place around, I just don't have the strength for it."

"I beg your pardon?"

Jon cupped her face in his hands and gently turned her to look at him.

"Now you listen to me. That is the daftest thing I've heard. You didn't bat an eye when you instructed the guy from Higson's where to stick his awful malt, did you? Not strong? I don't think so. You're strong enough to take on the running of a business, strong enough to sell off your country home to keep it going, and strong enough to lead all these men every day. You have an army of people who will go into battle for you— and therefore, this is a war your mother can never win."

"You think so?" she said shakily.

"I know so."

Desperate to ease her mind, he gave her a gentle kiss. She made no attempt to fight him off and instead melted into him and put her hands on the soft curve of his neck. He moved away after a while to see if she felt better.

"Will you do that again," she whispered before pressing her lips against his. He performed his duty without hesitation.

"You'll be fine. Please try not to worry. Come on, we'd better get back before my pa spots I'm missing again."

"Do you think he suspects? I do hope not."

"Ah, he just wants this pale ale order sorting. Don't you worry about a thing."

He grabbed the lantern and held it up alongside the creaky stairs so she could leave first.

"Go!" he whispered.

She gave him a smile and then disappeared back to her office.

Several times over the next few days, they would find some way to be alone together in some remote part of the premises. Each time they would swear not to do it again. Each time they met up again, they weakened to temptation.

Jon's grin had become a regular feature of his face. Never in his life had he enjoyed being so carefree and content. Word was starting to spread about his cheery mood.

Mrs Tucker, his next-door neighbour, gave him the third degree about it.

"My! You're looking in fine fettle, young Jon.
How's work going?"

When a shipment of the Pale Ale needed the customs paperwork to be dealt with, he bumped into Mr Sedgwick, the dock supervisor, and was met with a hug and a hearty slap on the back.

"We haven't seen you in ages! No doubt the reason
for your absence is worthwhile?"

After giving a wink and a sly tap on the nose, Sedgwick went off about his business.

Jon's father, ever watchful, was the first person to question him about her.

"Does that Stockwell woman have anything to do
with your rosy disposition?"

"Possibly," he replied.

Jon anticipated hearing a lecture and defending himself from a barrage of insults. Instead, David gave a little nod.

"Don't let me lose my job because of this, Jon.
Please? Think of the little 'uns?"

"Should something go awry, it will be me who finds
myself on my ear, not you."

"Well, I hope you're right. You're playing with fire,
boy. Are you serious about her?"

"Yes. I am sure she's serious about me too."

"You're kidding yerself. She doesn't have to give a
hoot. She could string you along as much as she

likes. She's the business owner. She's the one with the house in Mayfair. She's calling the shots here. You're the one who needs to dance to her tune. She could hint you need to be serious just to keep you sweet. Doing what she wants like a soppy little lapdog. Just be careful."

"It's not like I've proposed. We've had a few kisses down in the cellar and a few other quiet places here and there."

"Who's Jon been kissing?" Maggie teased.

"Come here, you little rascal!"

Jon leapt at her and scooped his little sister up into his strong arms. She wriggled and giggled as he plonked a big kiss on her forehead.

"I've been kissing you, Maggie Cavendish. Now, keep your beak out!" he said as he gently nuzzled her nose with his thumb and forefinger.

"Look! Look!" Rachel trilled from her usual spot by the window.

Jon went over to her, and they looked out together.

It was a dark, moonless night, the perfect backdrop for the first snow of the season to fall.

"I love the snow, me," David said from his place by the fire. "Always cheers me up to see those graceful little flakes giving the city a dusting like icing sugar on a cake."

"Yeah," Jon agreed softly, placing his hands on Rachel's little shoulders, but it wasn't her he wanted to hold onto.

How he wished Georgina was there to enjoy their first snowfall together. His heart ached to hold her close as they watched the snow gently fall from the sky.

His father's words had troubled him. What if he was a plaything for her, alright 'for now' but not 'forever.' How could he tell? It wasn't something he could ask her outright.

She seemed genuine enough when they were together, but when she was away in Mayfair with its late-night salons and cigar lounges, who knew what might be going on? She could bump into some charming industrialist her mother approved of and run off to his country house with him.

The minute he doubted her, he was crippled with guilt. How could he have thought such a horrid thing of her? She had given him no reason to doubt her. Perhaps his pa was meddling with his mind to get him to do what he wanted. It was all so confusing.

"I think I'll turn in, pa. It's been a long day."

18

CHRISTMAS IS COMING

Whitechapel prepared itself to bid November farewell and usher in December. Gusts of cold north-easterly wind buffeted the streets and signalled the start of the Christmas season. Shops and residences in the East End's poorest neighbourhoods started decorating their entrances and windows with whatever green foliage they could find, in keeping with the customs the Queen and her family established. The air was thick with the spicy aroma of freshly baked mince pies, yuletide logs, plum pudding, and other sweet holiday treats. The shop windows showcased an ever-expanding selection of novelties, curiosities, toys, books, and gifts.

This level of luxury was far beyond Jon and David's financial reach for many a year. But this year was different. Preparations began as soon as the family had a few pennies to spare.

The sack 'door' over the entrance to their lodgings had been upgraded to wood. For months they had begged their landlord Jimmy McGinty to fix it but had got nowhere. He was more interested in getting his workmen to put in dividing walls so he could up the rent. Regular maintenance work was a very poor second if it happened at all.

Jon brought home pretty pink-and-white striped paper bags full of mint humbugs or barley sugars. Maggie and Archie would shriek glee and stare wistfully at the modest collection when he appeared with them, and loved to wolf theirs down in one sitting. Rachel was more reserved with her rate of sweet consumption and made hers last for days.

David finally considered buying a goose to celebrate Christmas for the first time ever. He wasn't sure how he would get it cooked, but he vowed to investigate. There would also be lashings of Christmas cake and brandy butter.

It had been towards the end of November when Stockwell & Sons's festive ale was almost ready. After the small-scale tasting competition, the promising winning brew had gone into full production. It was a nervous time, but all the men watched the ale like hawks at every stage of manufacture, confident they had made the right choice. The stills were free of rust. Coming up with a hops-free recipe was a stroke of genius while the storage area in the warehouse dried out. Georgina had invested in the best metal barrels she could afford. Everybody was waiting to see how the finished product would taste with bated breath. The employees were invited to an exclusive launch party to have a tipple from the first few barrels. Colourful posters appeared at every railway and underground station. Boxes of colourful leaflets graced local shops' counters and the music halls' bars and entrances. More tasting parties were planned for the movers and shakers in the hospitality industry.

Georgina and Jon had worked with their printer to create an eye-catching, stylish festive label to adorn a small number of limited edition bottles destined for the food halls of middle-class department stores, upmarket hotels, cigar lounges and more.

For a few days now, Walter Sanders had checked the final brew in its huge cylindrical home. The other master brewers nervously gathered around him, as he prodded all sorts of new-fangled analytical instruments into it, and used time-old methods as he extracted numerous samples in a long glass flask, his skilled eye judging the depth of colour, his connoisseur's nose sniffing the aroma, his expert palate scrutinising the taste.

His conclusion of 'not yet, lads,' was met with downcast expressions. Jon began to worry if the brew would be ready for the launch party. It was cutting it fine. Next week was the first week of December.

Another three days later, the beer was ready to go into the casks, but it would be another day or two yet before it was prepared for a proper tasting session. Then, at last, the day came when the batch was finally finished.

At nearly seven in the evening, Walter announced the beer, cocooned in its shiny metal barrels, was at the proper temperature to be served. All day-shift men hung around, itching to try the much-touted beer and provide their opinion on it. Even Mr Bridges, a man who considered himself a white-collar professional, not a blue-collar ale-swilling type, stuck around, hanging back from the main group but still showing enthusiasm.

As the bells of St Matthew's chimed eight, everybody, including Georgina and Jon, congregated around three massive ale casks that had been ceremoniously carried up from the fermenting cellar. The whole place buzzed with excitement.

"Good job Mrs Stockwell got the steps repaired, eh, lads?" David Cavendish shouted. "I wouldn't fancy the chances for the old ones to support a chap carrying one of those up 'em. Three cheers for Mrs S! Hip! Hip!"

Thrice, the men whooped and hollered, whirling their caps in the air. Georgina blushed. The good thing was, the praise took her mind off the worry of how her latest ale would taste. What if it was awful? Then what? She decided it was best not to tempt fate and blanked her mind as best she could.

"Right. Sampling time. Who's going first?" Walter yelled over the chaos.

The men glanced about, with everyone wanting to offer but no one having the nerve to do it.

"Jon?" said Georgina.

"Me?"

His bravado seemed to melt away. He looked so taken aback.

"I think Eric should do it. He's a master brewer."

"You helped me develop the idea, Jon. You're our head of sales. And, of course, we all know you see yourself as a bit of an aficionado—"

The men whooped again as he humbly bowed his head.

"Come on. Someone's got to go first." David Cavendish chimed in with some words of support.

"Do it!" shouted Water Sanders, "you know what the punters want, and the landlords. Don't keep us waiting in suspense, lad."

It didn't take long for the others to agree, and soon Jon was being dragged to the front.

"Now, I want you to be honest, mate," warned Walter. "Speak up. If it needs more work, we need to know. No point in sparing anyone's feelings by being polite. A lot is riding on it. Sup up!"

Sanders removed the lid and opened up the bung. He slid a mug-style pint glass under a stream of ruby-black liquid, tilting it slightly. As the glass filled, a thick creamy head formed on top. The men jostled shoulders as the onlookers pressed in nearer and nearer.

"Well, gentlemen, it certainly looks ok," whooped Georgina, squished into the front row.

Sanders passed the glass to Jon, who reluctantly accepted it, conscious of the curious gazes of his father, the employees, and of course, 'her'.

"Cheers!" he yelled before he took a giant gulp from the glass.

He stood motionless, apart from his cheeks and lips swirling the liquid round, followed by a leap from his Adam's apple. The first mouthful of Stockwell's flagship festive ale had finally been swallowed.

The flavours delighted him. The bitter, hefty malt was a nice contrast to the delicate note provided by the cloves. The juniper contributed a distinctive Christmassy flavour that lingered on the palate. In addition, the strength of the alcohol was noticeable without being overbearing. In a nutshell, it was perhaps the best stout he'd ever tasted. It had everything they wanted from it: the solid backdrop of their top-quality stout, with the unique yuletide flavour they needed to pique the interest of their former loyal drinkers, and give the brewery one last try to redeem itself.

He kept his face deadpan, loving the way the men were on tenterhooks. He took another long, slow sip and eyed the brew to heighten the tension.

"Well?" asked Mr Bridges, all the way at the back, looking on in wide-eyed fascination, his hands placed over his heart to try and calm its rhythmic racing beat.

Jon grinned.

"It's a beaut, lads. A beaut! Oh—and lady. Sorry, Mrs Stockwell. It's even better than I imagined it could be."

The factory exploded with relief and joy. The men jumped, hugged each other and cheered. It looked more like a scene from the football terraces when the winning goal was scored.

Walter and Eric started filling glasses as fast as they could. The hasty pouring made the heads on each pint get thicker and thicker. No one cared. The pints were passed amongst the men like firemen handing filled fire buckets down the line, except quite a few surreptitious slurps were taken from the pints as they travelled.

Georgina made her way to David Cavendish.

"Would you mind bringing up a few barrels of our regular ale, please? These men deserve a few pints on me."

"Certainly, Mrs Stockwell," David said with a smile. "My pleasure."

The beer flowed freely. Laughter and merriment filled the room, soon to be replaced with off-key singing and clapping as the men danced jigs to the caterwauling.

For everyone, it was a true 'once in a lifetime' kind of night. Jon was ecstatic, as were all the others. Georgina joined in the party, singing and dancing with the men. She sipped at another glass of the Christmas Ale. When she noticed Jon looking at her, he winked, and she swung her half-empty glass in the air with pride. He moved to be nearer to her.

"I think it's gone well. If this doesn't save Stockwell's, then nothing will."

Mr Bridges interrupted them.

"Mrs Stockwell, Mr Glazer is waiting for you outside. He wanted you to know it was nearly half past ten."

Her face fell, and her loosened tongue mourned having to leave so soon.

"Oh, Jon, I'm not ready to go. We've all worked so hard. We deserve a little celebration."

"Then stay?"

"I daren't. Fighting off the continual threats from my mother is tough enough as it is! Staying out late with the men will only fan the flames and give her more ammunition to attack me with."

"How about we pay for a coach to take you home later?"

She shook her head sadly.

"Just an hour later?" he begged before suggesting. "Or I could also walk you home again? If you would like?"

"Thank you, but I don't want to do any of those."

"Oh," he lamented. "Shall I ask Mr Bridges to fetch your coat?"

"There's no need to be hasty," she said with a grin. "How about a hotel? I could get a room, say I was working late to finalise some information Mr Bridges needs. Mother knows he is terribly dull, always staring at documents."

"I am not sure a hotel in the East End is a good idea."

"No? Surely they can't be that woeful. As long as the door locks, I'll be happy."

"No, you don't understand. How shall I put this? They tend to be rented by the hour more than the night."

"Oh! Can you suggest something suitable a little further away, perhaps nearer St Pauls? I am sure I've seen some places near Ludgate Circus?"

"Perhaps," he said with his usual charming grin.

Could she really be suggesting what he thought she was suggesting? After the days of secret spine-tingling kisses, did she want more? Or did she just want more of his company? Maybe she just wanted to celebrate their months of hard work turning the business around.

"I know just the place."

"Excellent. Please accompany me with Mr Glazer. You can drop me off, then come back to the party. Then perhaps return to the hotel later?"

His heart thumped, and his mouth went dry.

"If that's what you want, then yes, of course."

"It is what I want. Can you go and get some box files? I shall tell Glazer I am reviewing the delivery schedule for the first samples due to be on the drapers' carts at five am tomorrow, and that it is not worth me going home."

"Will he believe you?"

"I doubt it," she whispered. "But frankly, tonight? I don't care. I have earned a celebration."

As Jon had guessed, Glazer was even less enthusiastic about taking the lady of the house to a hotel, than he was about having Jon walk her home earlier in the year.

Annoying as he was, Jon begrudgingly respected her coachman and his protective nature. After all, he would want to ensure Mrs Stockwell checked in to a respectable place too.

Georgina entered the carriage and offered a cheery greeting. She made a point of asking Glazer to stow the box files securely, even though he didn't look convinced in the slightest that she needed to review their contents.

"Mr Cavendish will explain where the hotel is."

Jon climbed alongside her driver to a distinctly frosty response.

The Leonardo Hotel was a down-at-heel but trustworthy establishment. It was the sort of place merchants would stay when doing deals down at the docks, or visiting clerics would stay on at conferences held near the cathedral. It was certainly too expensive for the lower-classes to use it by the hour. Although he had never stayed, he had done a few stints as a night watchman when the regular chap, the owner's distant relation, went away to fight a problem at one of his other hotels. In the dead of night, Jon would watch all the comings and goings and make sure none of the guests were rowdy, or the hotel's valuables were stolen.

"Well?" Georgina demanded as her frustration grew, with Glazer shadowing her every move. "Does this meet your exacting standards? Will you be able to report your satisfaction back to my mother and Mr McKay? I know you will."

"I suppose," said Mr Glazer, as he locked the door and then tugged at the handle. "I will come and collect you if you need me. Just send a runner with a message."

"Please. Will you stop fussing, Glazer? Now get along and take Mr Cavendish back to the celebrations. I have work to do."

As Glazer and Jon walked back to the coach, the driver gave him a stark warning.

"I will hold you alone responsible if anything happens to Mrs Stockwell. I know where you live."

The only sound was their footsteps as they made their way outside.

As Jon got into the coach, Glazer snarled, "Anything! You hear me?" to emphasise his point.

Jon suspected he had more in mind than her getting into bother with an intruder at the hotel.

"I'd expect nothing less," Cavendish replied with his best smile.

"Oh, Mr Glazer!" a voice called out. "Just before you go—"

He turned to see Mrs Stockwell on the front steps. His delight that she had changed her mind about staying was misguided.

"Would you mind asking Sarah to fix my blue dress? I was a little clumsy and got caught on a bit of metal yesterday, and it got a small tear near the hem."

Glazer gave a brief head-bob, cracked the reins, and the carriage started to move. Jon Cavendish slipped out of reach and out of view.

19

THE PARTY

When Jon got back to the party, it was still in full swing.

"Do you think this new ale is going to work like gangbusters, Mr Cavendish?" chirped Mr Bridges, who, to Jon's astonishment, seemed uncharacteristically animated.

"Oh, it'll work. I'm betting my future on it, ain't I."

"I suppose you are."

"I've softened a few of the old buyers up, as has Georgina. I have lost count of the number of times she's apologised to folks for Mr Duffield's shady shenanigans. How she keeps bowing and scraping to these people week in and out for a problem of her brother's making, well, it's nothing short of amazing."

"Quite," said Mr Bridges, taking another big swig of ale.

Jon rocked on his heels and grinned as he poured a pint for himself.

"Truth be told, I assumed those posh folk would always look out for their own. Mrs Stockwell's not defended him once. Hung him out to dry, she has - but she was very complimentary of all of us.

Honestly, she claims I'm supposed to be the chatterbox around here, but she's actually the one who's done the bulk of the talking."

"While I haven't known her for long, I confess, I admire her," Mr Bridges slurred. "There is a sincerity about the woman. While she may not have had an initial interest in the business, she always made time to talk to the men and pass the time of day. And that includes me!"

"Have you been working here for a long time, Mr Bridges?"

"Since I left school. Ten years or more. I remember Mr Stockwell's first week shadowing his father. It was a sight to behold when the brewery was at its peak. Seeing things end the way they did with Mr Duffield at the helm was a painful experience."

"Just what sort of person was Richard? If I might ask? I didn't want to upset Mrs Stockwell by asking her, but I am curious."

Mr Bridges smiled at Jon in a way that made him feel self-conscious.

"A decent man from a family of self-made industrialists. Hard-working. Not as well-bred as his wife was, which Mr and Mrs Duffield were livid about. But despite their differences and difficulties, the two fell in love and married. As you know, when Mrs Stockwell feels like rebelling against her parents, she will find a way to do it."

The two men fell silent as Walter Sanders offered them a top-up.

"After Richard passed away, she was depressed for a very long time. However, she looks content now. Like she has a purpose again. Fire in her belly. Looks like she's doing fine without a man at her side."

"That she is," said Jon. "She can hold her own amongst this rabble."

"Still, if the right man came along, she might weaken."

"I hope she doesn't have to settle for someone her parents choose for her," he said.

"Yes, not another chinless wonder like her brother. She needs an intelligent fellow. Someone with ambition? Perhaps someone of the merchant class?"

He gave Jon a nudge, making the man flustered and tongue-tied.

"I hope you're not suggesting a Whitechapel lad like me is one of those merchants, are ya? My neighbours would laugh me out of the tenement."

"What makes you think you're not, Mr Cavendish? You hold a responsible position here. The change in fortune has a lot to do with your tireless efforts. If I might speculate on Mrs Stockwell's take on this, based on how she conducts herself—a person's background doesn't matter, it's what they achieve."

Jon never considered himself one of the merchant class. All his aunts, uncles, and cousins were all day labourers. Only his father had a trade. He'd always considered himself a Whitechapel bloke, through and through, ducking and diving to eke out a living. But Mr Bridges was right. The position at Stockwell's was a golden opportunity for his silver tongue. And if anything ever happened to Stockwell's, another business would soon snap him up. His results for sales were stellar.

"Thank you, sir," came from Jon's lips. "Not many people believe in me. Your kind words mean a lot."

"What are you two up to?" asked Mrs Stockwell.

Jon whipped around, slightly startled but extremely pleased with Georgina's surprise appearance.

"Nothing, Mrs Stockwell," said a flustered Mr Bridges. "I have to go to the bathroom. Please forgive me."

"I got bored sat on my own, so I got the hotel manager to organise me a carriage. Another drink, Jon?" she asked as Sanders handed her a pint of porter.

"No thanks. I've had enough for tonight. I'll end up tipsy like my pa, warbling and waltzing like a court jester."

"I must say this ale is very—satisfying—" she said as she moved close enough to brush against him, then let her hand touch his stubbly chin.

Jon looked around nervously, worried that someone had witnessed her flirtatious gesture. The nudges, nods, winks and reprimands he received whenever her name was mentioned in the same sentence as him, was beginning to concern him. Thankfully, the men were having too much fun to notice.

"In a similar vein, I enjoy it. However, I, too, have consumed my fill. The next fortnight will be extremely hectic, and I need to keep a level mind. How do you feel about the launch, Jon? How will it go?"

"I am sure things will be fine. And if we hit a snag? Well, we can solve it together, like we always do," he reassured.

"I think we might be more prepared for what lies ahead, more ready for it than we think?"

"You might be right there, Georgina."

She looked up at him, her eyes twinkling. Jon wanted to seal the declaration with a passionate kiss, but he restrained himself. She glanced around and then stood on her tiptoes to give him a peck on the cheek, but he managed to resist.

They stayed until the clock struck midnight. The men were very much worse for wear by then.

"Come on now, lads, time for bed. We've got work to do tomorrow," Jon shouted as he walked amongst them. "Chop, chop!"

He walked over to Mr Bridges, who was dozing off in the corner on a crate and gently shook his arm.

"Up you come, Mr Bridges. You'll get a stiff neck falling asleep there."

"You're a good 'un, Jon. I'll see you bright and early."

"You will not," said Georgina. "I don't expect to see you before noon, Mr Bridges."

"But—!"

"No buts. I have processed all the paperwork for the sample deliveries. It's with the cartmen now. They're stacking as we speak."

"It's probably time for me to take you to your accommodation for the night too, Georgina," said Jon. "All sorts of dodgy types come out this time of night."

"If you must," she conceded. "I'll just get my coat."

She hurried up the flight of steps and swooped down with the coat flapping behind her.

When they got a few hundred yards from the brewery, they strolled close to one another, arm in arm, without caring whether anyone saw them. No one knew them there, so what did it matter?

London's terrible poverty was evident all around them, and a woman of Georgina's pedigree ought to have been horrified by what she witnessed. However, she didn't seem to notice the painted ladies loitering on the street corners, nor the gin-addled men haggling over the price for their services.

Usually, at this hour, those women would be swarming around a handsome man like Jon, begging him to seek their company in exchange for a few shillings or, if they were desperate enough, a cup of gin. But tonight, he was with Georgina. Having such a stunning woman on his arm was a waste of their time. Tonight, he was hers, and hers alone.

They strolled down Ludgate just as the snow began to fall again. The light flurry from yesterday had already melted. The flakes twirled about them. Like two children, they looked skyward, open-mouthed, trying to catch a flake and giggling when they did.

Georgina looked over at Jon as they approached the hotel, and he hoped to steal another sweet kiss. What happened instead surprised him.

"I don't want you to go home, Jon."

The comment caught his attention. Had he heard her properly?

She read his mind and put him in the picture.

"Yes. I want you to accompany me up to my room."

"Oh, Georgina... you know I want you more than anything in the world, But are you sure? You're a lady, after all. If someone found out, people could make your life a misery."

"Who would know?"

Jon looked all around. Everyone was hunched over, pulling their collars up under their chins, scuttling back to their warm homes.

"I'm really not sure about this."

"Jon," she urged with some frustration. "I was a married woman. I am now a widow. I am not a debutante in her first season."

"Gosh, absolutely", he replied without any hesitation, but he secretly wished he had held back a little for the sake of his own dignity.

Georgina took hold of his hand and tugged it towards the door. The concierge said nothing as they walked across the foyer to the stairs. Once out of sight, she turned and kissed him passionately, running her hands over his clothes, feeling his muscular body beneath.

"I'm sorry, I can't," he said, wriggling away.

She looked hurt, angry even.

"Why does everyone think they can control what I do with my life? Don't I get a say?"

He took her by the shoulders and looked her in the eye.

"I promised my father I would treat you with respect. Be a gentleman. Not do anything to rock the boat. My heart aches just to look at you. There is nothing more that I want—but I can't betray my word to my father. If I knew this was going to happen, I might not have made the promise to my pa, but I did."

She looked downhearted but respected his wishes, and he walked her to her door in silence, squeezing her hand tightly. He'd resented his father when he first brought up the subject of Georgina. Now he was grateful. It wouldn't be his first time with a woman if he stayed, but it had been a while. When things did move on, Jon was determined to make it very special.

As he kissed her goodnight at her doorway, she pulled at him, urging him to stay. He used all his willpower to break away.

"Goodnight, Georgina, my love. I shall see you tomorrow."

He watched her close the door. She flopped on her bed and clutched the spare pillow tightly to her body, wishing it was him.

20

SINK OR SWIM

Georgina was awakened from a heavenly slumber by the bustle of activity outside the window. Her eyes widened in the dreary morning light. It appeared to have been snowing for quite some time outdoors. Thick flakes floated lazily through the windows and piled up on the sill. The fire was just about still aglow in the hearth.

She clung to the pillow again, wanting Jon to be there to reassure her. Today, samples of Stockwell's Christmas Ale were going to all the department stores and restaurants. She worried, telling herself impressing the staff meant nothing. They were biased. It was strangers that needed to be won over.

She got out of bed and dressed hurriedly, then walked down the hallway. She asked for a carriage and then went to wait at the front of the building. As she stepped on the pavement, she froze and then tried to dart into a nearby doorway, pressing her back against the wall. *'Good Lord, help me.'*

"Georgina? Is that you?" shrieked Mrs Duffield. "I had heard you spent the night at this hotel. I had to see for myself. Butler told me. It seems he was telling me the truth! He said a man from the brewery was in tow. I do hope he is not here!"

Her mother's voice was filled with hatred.

"He's not. You can check if you like."

"Don't get clever with me."

"Mother, please. I worked till late yesterday night as the new festive ale was ready for tasting. The men said it was good enough to be put on sale. I didn't want to keep Glazer waiting while we discussed the minutiae of the project, nor expect him to drive me to Whitechapel at five in the morning to drop off some delivery instructions. It was noisy in the brewery, and I wanted somewhere quiet to work. This place suited my needs perfectly."

"Quite rightly, Mr Glazer had serious concerns. Georgina, I'm embarrassed by you. According to Mr McKay, this is the same man who barged into your home when you hosted James's party. And you've been secretly meeting with him, going to pubs with him in the evenings. How can you consort with a violent, repulsive creature from London's seedy underbelly? I can't understand you. Why do you insist on disgracing our family?"

"He's not a creature. He has helped save the brewery. The brewery that your precious son ran into the ground to fund his drinking and womanising. Don't talk to me about humiliating the family. James's lewd and selfish behaviour has made a mockery of the Duffield and Stockwell names the length and breadth of Britain. Mr Cavendish has helped me change those opinions, and it has been hard work! Believe me."

"He is a filthy creature if I say he is. And Mr Bainbridge has informed me that you've turned down his suggestions for a new man to come in and be the manager. He put in a lot of effort to find capable, honest men to take over your role, and you threw it back in his face, preferring to stay in post yourself and have this Cavendish fellow as your right-hand man. You couldn't have put poor Bainbridge's nose more out of joint if you'd spat in his face when you rejected all his efforts to help."

"I don't want a manager. I don't need a manager. I am the manager. Me. One glance at the balance sheet proves I am the right person for the job. Bainbridge can't argue with cold hard numbers."

Mrs Duffield grabbed Georgina by the elbow and dug her fingers in so hard the girl's arm ached.

"I can't take any more of this. You are coming back home right now. I'll discuss your wilful insubordination with your father and figure out how to repair the harm you've done to the family name by associating it with the lowest of the low of Whitechapel."

Georgina was gritting her teeth ever more tightly for fear of giving her mother a piece of her mind about how much nicer a person Jon was when compared to a shrew like her.

"We'll figure out our plans for the brewery after that. Selling it seems the best way to sever all ties with the area. And it's hardly a cash cow. You've had to sell one of your properties to prop it up. If your father can salvage the situation by selling the

business, you can use that money to support
yourself until we find you a husband."

Mrs Duffield tried to drag her daughter towards the coach. Glazer stepped down to reinforce his mistress's will. Georgina was in a panic. Everything she had grown to care about was about to be taken away from her. Her freedom to pursue her potential, follow her own interests, make something of the brewery, and follow her heart, was all hanging in the balance.

Her heart banged. Her throat felt like sandpaper. Her knees knocked.

"No," she responded, stamping her foot on the
ground, her arms stiffening at her sides.

"I will not discuss this here, Georgina. We are
going home this instant!"

Her mother's pincer-like grip swooped towards the girl, but like one of the ragged children in Whitechapel dodging a clip round the ear, she wriggled out of the way,

"You might be keen to go home. I am keen to go to
my workplace."

A few people were starting to gather around the feuding women. The concierge came to see what all the fuss was about and noticed Georgina looking flustered.

"Everything alright, Mrs Stockwell? Did your
carriage not arrive? The carriage you ordered to
take you to the brewery?"

"Why, I'm not sure. I was so preoccupied chatting
here on the street I forgot to look out for it. I'll

come inside and wait for another. If you don't mind?"

"My pleasure," said the smartly uniformed man as he manoeuvred himself between the two warring women.

Mrs Duffield glared at her daughter.

"You do realise this means giving up your father's financial support?"

"Is that the level we have sunk to? Trying to control me by cutting off my allowance?"

Mrs Duffield broke with protocol and poked her face into the side of her daughter's head, still trying to summon her back to Mr Glazer and the coach.

"A failing business and a failed Whitechapel wretch won't sustain you. After all the arguments about Richard, I thought you'd learned your lesson, but I was wrong. If that's what you want, Georgina, then that's your choice."

"Mother, when will you accept that Stockwell & Sons is no longer failing?"

Her mother scoffed, and Georgina resisted the strange urge to punch her.

"It's true. Steadily, we're getting more orders, our quality is improving, and we are about to launch a brand new limited edition ale. The staff and I have worked long and hard to make sure we improve, and we will. We are a team that pulls together. So

go ahead and cut me off, you and Father. I don't
need any money from you."

Her mother's mouth dropped open.

"And as for Mr Cavendish, he is a very clever man.
He has more ambition than James ever did. He may
not have been born into the best family, but it is a
loving family. He is proud of his family, and so am
I. Once he was given a chance, he thrived, and the
brewery thrived. And that makes me love him. I
might even just marry him; if I did, it would be
because I love him with all my heart, just as it
would be to swing a wrecking ball through your
life. Do whatever you want. I don't need you, and I
don't care."

Georgina said nothing more and vanished into the hotel,
never wanting to see her harpy of a mother ever again.
Proudly, she floated along to the concierge's desk like a
feather, relieved to feel the lightness return, knowing her
mother was finally defeated.

"Thank you, sir", she said to the concierge, pushing
a crisp pound note into his hand.

"Any friend of Mr Cavendish's is a friend of mine,"
he said with a smile. "Now, shall we sort out this
coach to Whitechapel?"

Mrs Duffield looked shaken. Without another word, she
stomped to her carriage and closed the door.

"As far as I am concerned, she is dead to me, Mr
Glazer. We gave her everything, and this is how she
thanks us."

"Yes, ma'am," said Mr Glazer, obliged to agree with his mistresses' opinion at all times.

When Georgina arrived at the brewery, she sank into her chair and fumbled with the papers on her desk, unable to concentrate.

Footsteps sounded on the stairs as Jon slowly ascended. He pulled up a seat and sat in front of her, taking both her shaking hands in his. Cautiously, he searched her face for a sign of what she was feeling.

"I bumped into my mother when I left the hotel. It's a good job you weren't there. She said some terrible things about you. But rest assured, she won't be interfering in our lives again."

He noticed joyfully she said 'our lives', but let it go for a moment.

"Well, I'm impressed as anything. You had another showdown and triumphed! How do you feel?"

"I feel..." she paused, searching for the right words. "disappointed but liberated. I'm sure this isn't the last of it, but it's a start. Hey, she might even dread meeting me now. I'm her nemesis," she chuckled.

"Georgina, you said 'our' lives" he said, then bit his lip.

"I also told her I love you," she said matter-of-factly. "I hope it's not unrequited—?"

He didn't bother calming her concerns with words. Instead, he pulled her close to him and kissed her tenderly. Her hands took his in a vice-like grip.

"I love you, Georgina Stockwell," he breathed when the kiss ended.

He rested his forehead against hers.

"It started the moment I came home and found you sitting at Archie's bedside, telling him that story— and I've fallen more in love with you every day."

Georgina smiled, feeling self-conscious.

"Well... let's not get ahead of ourselves just yet. We've got work to do. It's launch day. You might feel differently if all we've done is for nought, and the business does fail after all."

"Never," Jon insisted. "And if it did, we might be poor as church mice, but we will be happy together. I've had loads of practice. I'll show you how it's done."

"I'm not sure 1 could return to an existence where I don't work," she teased.

"Come with me to the docks. I'm sure I could convince Mr Sedgwick to give you a bit of sweeping to do," he said, as they laughed together.

21

JOY AND HOPE FOR THE FUTURE

The Christmas brew was a huge success. All the staff would enjoy a marvellous Christmas, thanks to Georgina paying them for all the extra shifts. There was also an unexpected bonus payment distributed in a Christmas card to every employee's household. The Cavendishs decided to celebrate in style.

Just before noon on Christmas Day, David Cavendish returned to the lodgings, carrying a red-hot roast goose fresh out of Mr Horowitz's oven.

Maggie hopped up and down behind her father as he teased the bird out of its cloth cocoon, then tried to climb on the table.

"For goodness' sake, Maggie, Calm down!"

"But I've never eaten a bit of goose before. How can you expect me to be calm?"

"Is it ready, though?" Archie whispered next to Rachel. "Is it supposed to be that pale?

"I'm not sure," she said, replying in secret behind her hand.

Sitting at the family table with David Cavendish, Georgina sighed wistfully.

"It smells wonderful, better than what my cook used to make at home. And isn't it nice that we have one chair each, rather than one between us! And a proper door that locks."

Jon chuckled as he took a seat and admired the spread. It was modest yet delectable. After so many skipped meals for David and Jon, and chunks of bread for breakfast for the young ones, this was luxury.

David served out three pints of Christmas ale for the adults and some dandelion and burdock for the youngsters.

After placing the goose on the table, Jon positioned himself directly in front of it. The bird was examined grimly as he prodded it with a blunt knife.

He turned to Georgina looking worried.

"How do you carve a goose?"

"Well, for starters, I think you've got it upside down. Perhaps turn it over?"

He wrestled it round with his utensils and then set to work.

"I don't think you'll be getting a job at the Savoy, Jon," Georgina teased.

"I wouldn't know. I've never been," he replied playfully.

Jon grumbled and fought with the bird for quite some time, but all credit to the chap, everyone ended up with a decent amount of delicious meat on their plate. Rachel served out the roast potatoes, which were golden light and fluffy and earned her a lot of praise.

Across the table, Jon looked at Georgina. His heart felt the warmest it had ever been.

The guest of honour feasted with the family, tucking into goose with chestnut stuffing, rich eggnog, sticky plum pudding, tangy candied peel, crisp gingerbread men, and hot freshly baked mince pies, thanks to the generosity of David and Jonathan Cavendish.

A tiny fir tree that stood in the corner was the same as the one the royal family of Queen Victoria had, although probably smaller, Jon guessed. The girls had cut some snowflake decorations out of some old copies of the Pall Mall Gazette. The ceiling had been decorated with some coloured paper chains made by the menfolk. Tenement lodgings had never seemed so beautiful and welcoming.

They had enjoyed such a wonderful day together, from the service at St Matthew's, to the carol singing in the courtyard of Tyndale Hall led by Reverend Simon Bennett, and accompanied by the Salvation Army brass band, to sitting back in their chairs, with bellies full of food.

The gentle snowfall at night marked the end of a perfect day. Maggie and Archie stared out of the window, transfixed by it. Their awestruck looks stayed on their faces until they heard childlike laughter coming from the street below.

"Dad, that's Edgar and James!" Archie cried as he pointed down at them. "They're having a snowball fight. Please, can we join in?"

"Please, pa!" Maggie squealed before stuffing a whole mince pie in her mouth.

Mr Cavendish finally gave in.

"Perhaps we should all go?" Jon suggested with a wink.

The household wrapped up warm in their coats and walked out into the courtyard.

The kids were running around amok. The snow brought some cheer into the hearts of even the poorest of kids, and their parents and grandparents too. It gave them so much joy to see the children this happy.

Archie's poor aim with his snowball meant Georgina got hit in the back of the head rather than his sister. The poor lad looked terrified as Georgina mouthed, 'Why, you little—.'

Before the boy could work out what was going on, she scooped up a handful of snow and lobbed it at Archie. As it hit him in the shoulder, she gave a massive whoop and started jumping about with glee. Eventually, Georgina's delight at snowball fighting gave way to some canoodling with Jon when no one was looking. They made such a romantic couple, facing each other, their foreheads touching and fingers entwined as the snowflakes fell all around them.

"You know, Jon. My house in Mayfair is far too big for me on my own."

"Is that so, Georgina?"

"And the journey to the brewery is longer than I would prefer."

"You've always told me 'it's just five miles,' whenever I said it was too far."

"Well, yes, five miles isn't that far, but it is when you need to do it twice a day. You see... I was considering moving a bit nearer."

She paused, looking up at him from beneath her lashes.

"Something with five bedrooms and enough room for a three- and a five-year-old to run around. Somewhere where neighbours moving in from Whitechapel won't be looked down upon."

"Are you asking me to marry you?" Jon teased.

"Certainly not. I might be a bit of a tomboy, but I will still wait for you to ask me. I am just being practical. Maggie and Archie need proper rooms. And Rachel, well, she's rapidly becoming a grown woman."

"That she is," Jon agreed. "And she'll need a good woman to model herself on."

Jon tightened his arms around her.

"Sharing a house together seems ideal, doesn't it?" she asked sweetly.

"It would be better than that. It would be perfect. Now, about that question—"

"How about you hang onto that question for just a while longer, Jonathan Cavendish," she said as she rested her head on his shoulder and gazed across at the children. Surprise me with it when I'm least expecting it."

He pressed his lips to the top of her head and kissed her fondly.

"It might mean no pints of ale down the pub after work. I will have quite a few lean weeks ahead as I save up to buy a ring. I am poor, you know."

She laughed and swatted him affectionately.

"I don't care one jot if you're poor, you idiot. So, it's settled. 1 shall look for a house closer to the brewery, and you shall continue to save your money."

"Agreed."

Together, blissfully, they watched the scene in the snow. David crawled around like a horse with Maggie and Archie on his back. As the sky cleared, the light from the full moon made the snow seem an even more perfect white.

Jon held her close as his mind drifted off to ponder the final gift he had for her. He and his father had pooled their bonuses to get it. They had been so busy enjoying themselves that he'd not given it to her that morning.

In his inside pocket were two gold rings in a delicate organza bag. Jon was no longer quite so poor as he was letting Georgina believe.

When he walked her home tonight, he would pop the question. Their first joyous Christmas of many to come would go down as their most memorable ever.

———

Enjoyed Georgina's Christmas Joy? Here are some more books in my 'Victorian Whitechapel Girls' series you'll love. Have you read them all?

- https://mybook.to/WhitechapelGirls

GET ONE OF MY BOOKS FREE

Hi! Beryl here.

You can download your free book here.

- [From Slum Girl to Country Maid](dl.bookfunnel.com/2jkv8e1qoq)

(dl.bookfunnel.com/2jkv8e1qoq)

Thanks for all your support. It means everything to me.